ST

They all shook hands, and as Carrie and Renee got up to leave, Renee asked, "Whose video is this? I mean, whose record is the video based on?"

Mac and Mrs. Haines exchanged looks.

"I wondered when one of you would ask that," Mac said. "OK, girls, are you ready?"

Names of rock groups and singers flashed through Carrie's mind. She'd be excited to work with any of them. But she wasn't prepared for the thrill that ran through her when she heard Mac's next words.

"You girls will be appearing in a new video with Michael Jackson!"

Star Struck!

Shannon Blair

BANTAM BOOKS
TORONTO · NEW YORK · LONDON · SYDNEY · AUCKLAND

RL 5, IL age 11 and up

STAR STRUCK!
A Bantam Book / March 1985

ISBN 0-553-24971-1

Published simultaneously in the United States and Canada

---

*Bantam Books are published by Bantam Books, Inc. Its trademark,
consisting of the words "Bantam Books" and the portrayal of a
rooster, is registered in U.S. Patent and Trademark Office and in
other countries. Marca Registrada. Bantam Books, Inc., 666 Fifth
Avenue, New York, New York 10103.*

Printed and bound in Great Britain by Hunt Barnard Printing Ltd.

O   0 9 8 7 6 5 4 3 2 1

To Susan Smith, who listened.

Chapter One

Carrie sat on the bare studio floor and stretched her arms in the general direction of her toes. She was pleased to find she could do this much more easily than she could three weeks before when she had first started taking jazz dance classes.

She was glad she had decided to do something different for the summer. When school let out just a month earlier, she was feeling pretty down. She hadn't made the cheerleading squad. That particularly hurt since her best girlfriends, Amy and Susan, had tried out with her, and they had made it. But it didn't really surprise her that she wasn't chosen; she'd never been very graceful or any good at gymnastics. But this meant Amy and Susan would be practicing a lot over the summer, and Carrie wouldn't have anyone to hang around with. The other blow came when her mother had announced that they wouldn't be spending their usual three weeks in August at the beach. She had just started a new job, and she wouldn't have any vacation time until Christmas. Carrie would be stuck in her suburban Los Angeles home all summer.

When her mother saw the ad for beginning dance classes in the newspaper, she brought it to Carrie's attention. At first Carrie wasn't very excited.

"Mom," Carrie complained, "I don't want to be a dancer."

"That's not the point," her mother argued. "It's good exercise, it's healthy, and it'll get you out of the house. Besides," she added gently, "maybe if you improve your coordination, you could make the cheerleading team next year when you're a junior."

She was right, and Carrie knew it. She had pretty much resigned herself to a summer of reading, watching TV, and listening to records, and none of that was very exciting.

The dance classes had turned out to be OK. She wasn't a particularly good dancer, but the other girls in the class seemed nice, and the routines they were learning were fun to do.

A tall, pretty girl in a purple leotard, Julie Lyons, flopped down next to her and began doing the same exercise. She seemed to be out of breath.

"I thought I was going to be late," she confided to Carrie. "I had an audition this morning for a commercial, and I had to wait a half hour before I was seen!"

Carrie self-consciously adjusted the straps of her own plain, black leotard and wished for the zillionth time that her figure wasn't so, well, underdeveloped.

"Did you get the job?" she asked curiously.

Julie smiled and shrugged. "Don't know," she said. "Probably not. You wouldn't believe how many pretty girls there are in L.A., and they all want to be models and actresses."

"Still, it must be exciting," Carrie said as she pushed her short, dark curls away from her face. "I mean, being a professional actress is so glamorous."

Julie laughed. "I'm not really a professional, yet. But I will be! And I figure I've got time. After all, I'm only sixteen."

Carrie was surprised. She herself was

going to be sixteen in September. This sophisticated-looking girl was practically the same age she was!

"It does seem like just about everyone in this class is trying to be a model, an actress, or a dancer," Carrie remarked.

"Which are you?" Julie asked.

Carrie laughed. "None of the above. I'm just trying to be less of a klutz. I want to make the cheerleading squad at my high school." She felt a little silly saying this. Cheerleading must sound pretty dumb to an aspiring actress. But the blond girl nodded approvingly.

"Dance classes are good for improving coordination," she said. "I wish I could go out for cheerleading at my high school. But I'm always running around to auditions, and I never have time for school activities."

The room was beginning to fill up with girls, who were chattering, laughing, and stretching.

"Now there's a girl with natural grace," Julie murmured, indicating an extremely pretty girl with long, fair hair who was practicing leg lifts at the bar. Carrie tried to avoid making a face.

"That's Renee Mitchell," she said. "She

goes to my high school." She didn't go on to add that Renee was one of her least favorite people. She was the type who went after every good-looking boy in school—and usually got them.

The teacher, Mrs. Haines, walked in then, and the girls quieted down. Carrie admired the grace of the elegant, slender, middle-aged woman as she strolled across the room, talking quietly with a short, slightly pudgy man in a business suit.

"There's that Mr. MacDonald again," a voice behind Carrie whispered. Carrie glanced over her shoulder and noted, with some dismay, that Renee was standing directly behind her. She didn't like the idea that Renee would be observing her own slightly gawky attempts at kicks and spins.

But Carrie had to admit that she, too, was curious about the mysterious Mr. MacDonald. Mrs. Haines had introduced him to the class, but she didn't say what he was doing there. He was obviously not a dancer. He'd been observing the class for two days now, sitting silently in a corner and occasionally talking very quietly to Mrs. Haines.

"Who is he, anyway?" Carrie asked Renee in a whisper.

Renee shrugged. "I don't know," she said, "but I think, maybe, he might be a movie producer looking for new talent. You know Mrs. Haines used to dance in the movies."

Carrie remembered Mrs. Haines telling the class about her days as a chorus girl in movie musicals in the 1950s. She often wondered how a person could leave the glamour of Hollywood for a life as a dancing teacher in the suburbs.

She had a feeling that several other girls shared Renee's suspicions about Mr. Mac-Donald. Since he'd been observing the class, some of the more ambitious students had been knocking themselves out trying to do unbelievably complicated dance steps.

Not Carrie, though. To begin with, she knew she was definitely not one of the better dancers in the class, and that wasn't false modesty. And furthermore, although she admired, and even occasionally envied, the ambitions of some of her classmates, she had no interest in a performing career herself. Much as she liked reading about movie stars and rock stars in magazines, she knew that whatever talents she might have were not of the show biz variety.

Suddenly Renee was poking her shoulder,

trying to get her attention.. "Can I change places with you?"

Carrie turned. "Why?"

Renee looked impatient. "I need to be in the front row," she hissed. "I want this MacDonald guy to notice me."

Carrie rolled her eyes.

"Come on," Renee persisted. "If that man's really a producer, this could be my chance."

Carrie groaned, but she obliged and edged backward so Renee could move in front of her. *Might as well*, she thought to herself. *It's not as if a Hollywood producer would pay attention to me!*

"OK, girls," Mrs. Haines called out, "let's start with some aerobics." She put a cassette on the tape deck, and the driving beat of Michael Jackson's "Billie Jean" filled the room. The strong rhythm of the drums was accentuated by the sound of feet hitting the floor as the class erupted into jumping jacks.

"Arms to the side and twist," Mrs. Haines shouted. In front of Carrie, Renee was swinging her arms so wide she almost hit Carrie in the face.

"Watch it," Carrie muttered, but Renee ignored her.

"Now jog in place!"

The music was drowned out by the sound of stamping feet.

"Lightly, girls, lightly! Now slow down—and stop. Breathe in—and exhale. Very good. Now, let's go through the routine we learned yesterday. *And* step, step, kick, step, turn and one and two and one and two . . ."

Carrie went through the steps, counting softly to herself and trying not to look at her feet. It was a pretty easy sequence of movements. Glancing around the room, she noticed that Mr. MacDonald seemed to be looking intently at Renee. Then, for a moment, he seemed to have his eyes on Carrie.

"Now, double the beat, one, two, one, two . . ."

Carrie had to concentrate now, and she focused on Mrs. Haines. She was late on a turn and caught a glimpse of Renee's face as she whirled around. She had on this fake, too-too vivacious smile that Carrie had seen her use at school when she wanted to impress teachers or boys with her enthusiasm. *What a phony*, Carrie thought. But she had to admit that Renee was a good dancer. And she didn't even seem to sweat! Carrie was uncomfortably

8

aware of a trickle of perspiration running down her neck.

"Very good," Mrs. Haines called out. "Now, watch carefully. This is the next combination." With her arms extended, she gracefully executed what looked to Carrie like an incredibly complicated series of twists, kicks, and a deep lunge. Carrie's mouth fell open at the thought of trying to copy her. At least she wasn't alone in her reaction. Mrs. Haines's performance was greeted by a chorus of groans, and she smiled broadly.

"Yes, I know it looks difficult, but if you break it up into individual movements, you'll see that it's not impossible. It's the combination that makes the sequence seem complicated. Now follow me, and we'll go through each step slowly."

Carrie focused on Mrs. Haines and tried to make her feet follow what she was watching. Step, step, kick, hop, turn—and Carrie hit the floor.

She sat there for a second, trying to figure out how she'd managed to trip over her own feet. She could hear Renee's muffled giggles, and she flushed with embarrassment. But she managed a good-natured grin and bounced back up. As she did, she noticed that Mr.

MacDonald was looking at her. *I'll bet he's getting a good laugh*, Carrie thought. Strangely enough, though, his expression wasn't amused. Instead, he looked thoughtful. He beckoned to Mrs. Haines.

"OK, girls, try those steps on your own for a few minutes. Then we'll run through it again." She and Mr. MacDonald talked quietly, while the students worked alone or in small groups. Julie joined Carrie in a corner of the room.

"That was quite a fall you took," she said. "You didn't hurt yourself, did you?"

Carrie grinned ruefully. "No, I'm so used to stumbling, I think I've developed a thick skin."

"Let's go through these steps together," Julie suggested, and Carrie gratefully agreed. Working one to one made it all a lot easier, and Carrie was pleasantly surprised to find herself actually doing the sequence properly. When she finally reached a point where she could take her eyes off her feet, she saw Renee standing in front of her and smiling in a condescending way.

"That's not too bad, Carrie," she said.

"Thanks," Carrie said briefly. Renee's voice was mocking, but Carrie was not going to let it get to her. Julie had drifted away by then, and Carrie paused to take a breath before Mrs. Haines called the class back together. She wished Renee would vanish, but the girl just stood there with that amused expression on her face.

Unexpectedly Renee suddenly said, "I ran into a guy from school yesterday. Barry Gordon. Do you know him?"

"Yes," Carrie replied shortly. "I know him. What about him?"

"Nothing," Renee said. "It's just that I'd never really noticed him before. But he got the braces off his teeth, and he's really cute."

The way she said that made Carrie raise her eyebrows. "I know he's cute," she said. "He goes out with my friend Amy."

Renee's laugh wasn't very pleasant. "So what?" she said. "I mean, they're not married, are they?" And with that, she gave another little laugh and sauntered away. As Carrie made a mental note to warn Amy about Renee, Mrs. Haines clapped her hands.

"OK, girls, let's make two lines and go through this combination."

As Carrie moved to take her place in the line, she passed Mrs. Haines, who touched her shoulder lightly.

"Carrie," she said in a low voice, "would you stay for a few minutes after class?"

Carrie nodded and wondered what Mrs. Haines wanted with her. She noticed that the teacher was speaking to Renee, too.

The rest of the class went smoothly, and Carrie mentally patted herself on the back for managing to stay on her feet.

"All right, girls, thank you. That's all for today," Mrs. Haines said. "And I'll see you next class."

As the girls drifted out, Carrie lingered behind, and so did Renee. Mrs. Haines beckoned to them.

"Would you both come into my office," she said. It was more a statement than a question, and the two girls followed her silently.

Mr. MacDonald was waiting in Mrs. Haines's office.

"Carrie Philips, Renee Mitchell, this is Mr. MacDonald." The pudgy, pleasant-faced man shook hands with each of them.

"Call me Mac," he said and indicated that they should sit down. Carrie was completely puzzled. Who *was* this man, anyway? And what could he possibly want with her?

Mrs. Haines answered the first unspoken question.

"Mac and I are old friends," she said, smiling fondly at the man. "When I was dancing in the movies, back in the fifties, he was an assistant director. Now he's a full-fledged director."

"Do you direct movies?" Renee asked eagerly.

Mac grinned. "No," he replied. "I've never done a feature-length film on my own. Mostly I've been a director of commercials."

"Oh." Renee looked disappointed, but Carrie looked at the man with interest. She'd never met *any* kind of director before.

"Lately," Mac continued, "I've been directing music videos. I'm sure both of you are familiar with those."

Carrie nodded eagerly. She loved music videos; in fact, she'd had many arguments with her mother over the amount of time she spent glued to the TV station that played the videos all day. For Carrie, videos were an incredible combination of music, theater, film, dance, and art, and they really excited her.

"Which ones have you directed?" she asked curiously. Mac rattled off a few titles, and Carrie's eyes got bigger. "Those are some of my favorites!" she exclaimed.

Mac smiled. "Thanks," he said. "Personally, I think music videos are a dynamic new way to look at as well as hear music."

Carrie nodded enthusiastically and glanced to see Renee's response. The pretty girl had a peculiar expression—as if she was interested but trying to look nonchalant, even a little bored.

"I'm getting ready to start on a new video," Mac said. "It requires about a dozen people, teenagers, in various settings, like a classroom and a disco. I've been looking for two more 'extras,' as we call them, to be in certain scenes. Are you girls interested?"

Carrie's mouth fell open. She looked at Renee and saw that the mask of nonchalance had fallen from her face. Renee, too, looked stunned.

"But—" Carrie fumbled for the words. "I mean—me? I'm not a very good dancer."

Mac shook his head and smiled.

"I'm not looking for dancers," he said. "There's very little dancing involved, except in the disco scene, and that will be very simple. What I'm more concerned with is a certain look. I want kids, excuse me, young adults, who have a natural, clean-cut look. No glamour girls, no—pardon the expression—

sexpots. I want pretty young women, good-looking young men, who will fit in with the kind of image this video will project. And you two girls look exactly right."

Carrie didn't know what to say. She looked at Renee.

"What would we have to do?" Renee asked.

"It's a lot of hard work," Mac said. "Although if I describe the video to you now, it's going to sound very easy. I'm asking all the extras to meet with me Thursday at the studio, and I'll explain it all to you then. But I've watched you both the past two days, and I can tell you that I feel very certain you'll be able to do what I want."

There was a silence in the room as both girls contemplated this amazing offer.

"By the way," Mac added, "if you'll give me your phone numbers, I'll be happy to talk with your parents about this. Of course, you will both receive an appropriate remuneration for your work."

Renee's face went blank, and Mac defined that. "I'm talking about a salary. I'll discuss that with your parents."

Carrie was still stunned, but she was aware of a tingle running through her. *She* was going to appear in a music video! And get *paid* for it!

She was barely aware of the next few minutes. The girls wrote down their phone numbers, and Mac told them where they were to report on Thursday. It was a big movie studio in Hollywood.

They all shook hands again, and as Carrie and Renee got up to leave, Renee asked, "Whose video is this? I mean, whose record is the video based on?"

Mac and Mrs. Haines exchanged looks.

"I wondered when one of you would ask that," he said. "OK, girls, are you ready?"

Names of rock groups and singers flashed through Carrie's mind. She'd be excited to work with any of them! But she wasn't prepared for the thrill that ran through her when she heard Mac's next words.

"You girls will be appearing in a new video with"—he paused dramatically—"Michael Jackson."

Chapter Two

Carrie was still in a daze when she walked into her empty house almost an hour later. The walk home from the dance studio usually took her twenty minutes—but this time it was as if she had moved in slow motion. Mac's last words had left her feeling numb.

The thought of actually being in a music video was startling enough. But to be in a video with Michael Jackson? The hottest superstar in the entire world? The whole thing seemed unreal. For a fleeting second, Carrie wondered if she might have misheard Mac. But even in the fog that was surrounding her, the scene in Mrs. Haines's office *was* vividly impressed on her mind. She had to laugh as she tried to picture what her expression must have been like when Mac had said that famous name. Renee had looked as if she had gone into a state of total shock.

And for once, Carrie knew exactly what Renee was feeling.

She eased herself into a chair in the living room, sat very still, and stared into space. Somehow she still didn't believe this could all be happening. She, Carrie Philips, average fifteen-year-old girl, was going to be in a music video with Michael Jackson. It was totally awesome.

As she became a little calmer, she felt a burning desire to share this incredible news. She considered calling her mother and telling her, but decided to wait until she got home. She wanted to see her mother's expression. But maybe Amy and Susan would be free.

Her hands were trembling as she dialed Amy's number.

"Amy? Hi, it's Carrie." As the words left her lips, she was actually conscious of a tremor in her voice. Amy heard it, too.

"Carrie! Are you OK?"

"Oh, I'm OK," Carrie said. "But something really major has happened. Can you come over?"

Amy sounded concerned. "What happened? Are you sure you're all right? You sound strange."

Carrie tried to keep her voice under control. "I want to tell you in person. I'm going to call Susan, too."

"Susan's here," Amy said quickly. "We're on our way." And she hung up.

As she waited for her friends Carrie paced around the living room. She stopped in front of the stereo and thumbed through her albums until she came to Michael Jackson's *Thriller*. Carefully she pulled the record from the sleeve and laid it on the turntable. As the rhythm of "Beat It" filled the room, she tried to picture Michael in person, singing and dancing. . . .

Lost in a fantasy, she was only dimly aware of the doorbell. She floated to the door.

"Hi," she said dreamily to her friends. Amy and Susan eyed her uneasily as they walked in.

"What's going on?" Susan practically yelled.

Amy went over to the stereo. "Can I turn this down?" she shouted. "I mean, I love Michael Jackson, but I can't even hear my own voice!"

"Sure, turn it down," Carrie said, resisting an impulse to burst into hysterical giggles.

Her two best friends settled themselves into chairs and gazed at Carrie expectantly. Carrie had a sly urge to extend the suspense as long as possible. Amy's face reflected a mixture of concern and curiosity, and she tugged at her closely cropped black hair—a habit that Carrie knew meant she was worried. Susan looked solemn and tense. Her normally pale complexion was so flushed that Carrie could barely see the multitude of freckles that crossed her face.

Carrie grinned. "Hey, you guys, don't look so worried! It's good news! No, more than good—it's incredible!"

She watched two pairs of eyes get wider and wider. Only a short time before, they'd been looking at her with sympathy, when she was the only one of the three not to make the cheerleading squad. She imagined their expressions when they heard this news—what a difference!

"Ok, OK," Amy said impatiently. "I can't stand this any longer! What happened?"

Carrie took a deep breath. She had tormented her friends long enough.

"A director's been observing my dance

class," she said in a rush. "And he's asked Renee Mitchell and me to be extras in a music video."

Their mouths fell open simultaneously and then came a chorus of shrieks. Before they could respond any further, Carrie continued.

"Wait—you haven't heard it all. This particular music video features—a certain *major* recording superstar."

"Who?" asked her friends together.

Carrie grinned wickedly. "Guess."

The two girls groaned.

"OK," Carrie laughed. "Are you ready?" She paused dramatically, just as Mac had in Mrs. Haines's office. "It's Michael Jackson's new video."

She was completely satisfied with their reaction. Amy and Susan shrieked, screamed, and generally went nuts.

"Michael Jackson! You're going to see Michael Jackson! I can't believe it! He's so wonderful!" Suddenly the three of them were clutching one another's hands and jumping up and down. Then they all collapsed on the floor, giggling and gasping for breath.

Amy recovered first, and in her practical,

down-to-earth way, she wanted all the details. "What do *you* do in the video?" she asked.

"I haven't the slightest idea," Carrie admitted. "I'm supposed to go to a meeting on Thursday."

"Wow," Susan said, "that's the day after tomorrow. Gosh, do you think *he'll* be there?"

"I don't think so," Carrie replied. "This is just a meeting of the extras so we can find out what we're going to be doing. I guess he'll show up eventually, though. I mean, he *is* the star!"

"How come the director picked *you*?" Amy asked curiously. "Not that you don't deserve it," she added hastily. "But you said yourself, you're not a great dancer."

Carrie shrugged.

"Mac, that's the director, said I had the right 'look,' " she replied and struck a glamorous pose. The girls collapsed in giggles again.

"Who did you say the other girl was?" Susan asked.

"Renee Mitchell. You know her."

The expressions that greeted the name indicated that yes, both Susan and Amy knew her.

"She's so obnoxious," Amy said. "Why would the director want *her*?"

"I guess he's not interested in personalities," Carrie replied. "I mean, you have to admit she *is* pretty. Actually," she continued hesitantly, "I can't see why he picked me with Renee. I know I'm not ugly, but I'm definitely not in Renee's league."

"But you're cute," Susan said loyally. "And you're definitely more natural-looking than she is."

"Renee's a creep," Amy said flatly. "I hate the way she tries to collect boys—like they're stamps or something."

Something clicked in Carrie's mind. What was it she had made a mental note about? Then she remembered. She looked at Amy apprehensively.

"Renee told me she saw Barry the other day," she said. "And she went on about how cute he looks without his braces. I just thought I'd better warn you—"

Amy shrugged nonchalantly. "I'm not worried," she said. "I think Barry and I have a pretty good relationship." She paused, her eyes narrowing, and she added darkly, "But if she tries to stick her claws in him—"

"I wouldn't sweat it," Susan said comfortingly. "Once she's on that video set, she'll probably forget all about Barry and go after Michael Jackson!"

The thought of Renee chasing after the superstar sent the three of them into hysterical giggles again. Then Susan got a faraway look in her eyes—a look that Amy and Carrie knew very well.

"Or maybe," she murmured, "when Michael sees *you*, he'll look into your eyes and see the special someone he's been waiting for. And then he'll—"

She didn't get to finish her fantasy. In unison Carrie and Amy yelled "Su-san!" It was a familiar routine for all of them. Susan was the dreamy one, and Amy and Carrie were always having to bring her down to earth.

"Seriously, though," Amy said, "I'll bet there will be some cute guys there. Maybe you'll meet someone."

Carrie had been so overwhelmed by the idea of being in a video and meeting Michael Jackson, she hadn't even thought about the possibility of meeting anyone else.

"Gee, wouldn't that be great," she said. "Here I am, almost sixteen years old, and I've never had a real boyfriend."

"Well, let's face it," Amy said frankly. "You've always been pretty shy, and most of the guys at school think of you as sweet, little, ordinary Carrie. They take you for granted. Now you've got a chance to meet some new guys who don't have any preconceived notions about you."

Only a really good friend could say something like that and get away with it. But Carrie knew that what Amy said was true. She'd always wondered if she'd ever meet a boy who would see her as someone special, unique. She had a feeling that if a guy really tried to know her, he'd find out that she really wasn't so ordinary. But would any guy ever make the effort?

"I can see it all now," Susan said softly. "Your eyes will meet across a crowded room—"

"SU-SAN!"

They spent the rest of the afternoon watching videos on TV and hoping one of Michael's would be shown. When Carrie heard the door open, she jumped up.

"Wait till Mom hears about this!" she said and ran to the door to greet her. But the pleased expression on her mother's face made her suspect that she had already heard the great news. She was right.

"Darling, how exciting!" her mother exclaimed when she saw Carrie. "And I was afraid you'd have a boring summer! Hi, girls," she greeted the others. "Isn't this wonderful? Mr. MacDonald called me at the office, and we had a nice talk. This is going to be an incredible experience!" She reached into the bag she was carrying and lifted out a bakery box. "How about some brownies to celebrate?"

Later than night as she lay in bed, Carrie could finally take a deep breath and let her mind wander. Could this really be happening to her? She had never thought of herself as the kind of person exciting things happened to. At school she was a good student, but not brilliant. She had friends, and occasionally she even had dates, but she wasn't wildly popular. She thought she was reasonably cute, but certainly not gorgeous. Never, in a million years, could she imagine herself being singled out for such an honor. She felt so—special.

Her sleepy eyes turned to the poster of Michael Jackson hanging on her wall. It had been up there for months, along with the posters of half a dozen other rock stars. But now it took on a new meaning for her. Those deep, dark, serious eyes, that sweet, shy smile.

"I wonder what he's really like?" she asked herself as she drifted off to sleep. "Maybe I'll soon find out. . . ."

Chapter Three

When she woke on Wednesday, the main thing on Carrie's mind was clothes. It took ages for her to decide what to wear to the first meeting. She rummaged through her closet countless times. *It's just a meeting,* she kept telling herself, *and no one expects you to look like a movie star.* She finally settled on white jeans with a lemon yellow T-shirt. But by Thursday, the morning of the meeting, she had changed her mind half a dozen times before settling—again—on the same jeans and T-shirt. She checked out her reflection in the mirror and felt reasonably pleased with it. All right, she was no Renee Mitchell, but the pale yellow top set off the dark curls that framed her face. She'd managed, somehow, to get enough sleep, so she didn't have dark circles under her brown eyes. And, thank goodness, her complexion had been clear lately.

"I can drop you off at the studio," her mother said when they met at the breakfast table in the kitchen. "But how are you going to get home?" She looked concerned.

"I think there's a bus," Carrie said as she played with her cereal. She was definitely not hungry—her stomach was in knots. "Or maybe I can get a ride with Renee. Don't worry about it." Her mother still looked concerned, and Carrie assured her she'd call if she didn't have a way home.

Carrie had been to a movie studio once before, on a tour with her seventh grade class. But this was different. There was a guard at the gate where her mother stopped the car, and he asked for a name.

"I'm Carrie Philips," she said nervously. "I'm supposed to go to a meeting . . ." But the guard wasn't listening. He looked at a list he had, made a check with a pencil, then said, "Studio Seven-B," and waved the car through the gate.

Once inside the studio area, Carrie saw large white buildings that looked like warehouses lining the road.

"Why don't you let me out here and I'll find it," Carrie suggested. Her mother agreed, wished her luck, and Carrie hopped out. Crossing the road and rushing into and out of the studios were many actors and actresses in full costume—Roman warriors, cowboys, clowns. Long racks of clothes and bulky technical equipment were being wheeled by. Despite her nervousness and all the frantic movement around her, Carrie did manage to notice the abundance of really cute actors everywhere!

She located the studio easily and walked through the open barnlike door. The studio was a huge place, with incredibly high ceilings. There were great big cameras all around, and they cast eerie shadows on the walls. The floor was strewn with wires going every which way, and Carrie had to step carefully over and around them.

For a minute she thought the place was empty. She could hear the echo of her footsteps as she moved tentatively forward. Then she realized there were some people gathered at the far end of the room, and she recognized Mr. MacDonald.

She approached the group and stood there hesitantly. There were five or six kids sitting around, and most of them looked as if they were about her age. She didn't see Renee—the only time in her life Carrie was hoping to see her. Mr. MacDonald was talking to someone, and she didn't recognize anyone else. She was just debating whether or not to introduce herself to one of the other kids when a deep, friendly voice behind her said, "Hi, are you an extra, too?"

Carrie turned and looked up into a great pair of deep brown eyes. "Yes," she said. "I'm Carrie Philips."

"Joe Davenport," he replied and smiled a smile that rivaled his good-looking eyes. He had curly, dark hair, and a few curls fell casually over his forehead. Carrie gulped.

"Nice to meet you," she said as she frantically tried to think of something more to say.

"Is this your first time?" Joe asked.

"Huh?" Carrie responded, then wanted to kick herself for sounding so stupid. But Joe just smiled.

"Have you ever done this kind of work before?"

"No," Carrie said. "Never. Have you?"

Joe shook his head. "I've never worked on a video before. How did you get involved in this?"

Carrie told him about Mr. MacDonald observing her dance class and choosing her and Renee.

"He said there wouldn't be much dancing involved," she said uncertainly.

"I hope not!" Joe said, laughing. "I've never had a dance class in my life. Actually, I think the work mostly involves sitting around and making the right expressions—you know, looking good." He then looked at Carrie with frank appreciation. "That shouldn't be too difficult for you!"

Carrie could feel the blush creeping up her neck. She felt as though she were walking through one of Susan's fantasies!

"Uh, how did you get into this?" she asked quickly. Now Joe looked as if he were about to blush.

"Well, um, I sort of helped with the record for the video."

"How do you mean 'helped'?"

Joe gave her a half smile. "I was one of the back-up singers on the record."

Carrie's eyes widened. "You're a back-up singer? For Michael Jackson?!"

"Just on this cut," Joe added hastily. "I've been doing back-up work for about a year now, for different groups and singers."

Carrie was truly impressed. "That must be exciting!"

Joe shrugged lightly. "Sometimes it's fun, sometimes it's not. A lot depends on the people you work with. Some of these rock people can be pretty weird. The money's good, though, and I'm socking it away for college next year."

Carrie couldn't resist asking him what it was like working with Michael Jackson.

"He was OK. I didn't really get to know him, but he was always nice, very professional, and considerate of everyone else."

Even though Carrie was hanging on to every word, she noticed that Mac was arranging chairs in a circle. There were at least ten kids there now, standing, sitting, looking around uneasily. Carrie realized that she was twisting her hands together—her very own nervous habit. A good-looking guy with shiny blond hair approached them.

"Uh, does anyone know what we're supposed to be doing?" he asked.

"I think Mac's just waiting for everyone to get here so he can call the meeting to order," Joe said and put out his right hand. "I'm Joe Davenport, and this is Carrie Philips."

The boy introduced himself as Mark

Clinton. He was obviously trying to look casual and nonchalant, but Carrie could tell he wasn't feeling any more confident than she felt.

"OK, everyone, let's get started." Mac indicated the circle of chairs, and Joe, Carrie, and Mark moved toward them.

"Nervous?" Joe asked.

"Not really," Carrie lied. Then she grinned. "Well, maybe just a little."

Joe grinned back at her.

"There's nothing to be worried about," he assured her. "This could be a lot of fun. As long as you don't take it too seriously."

What an odd thing to say, Carrie thought. She wondered what Joe meant.

Chapter Four

The extras sat down. Carrie looked around the circle and counted eleven of them—five girls, six boys. She was glad to see that just about all of them had on jeans and T-shirts. She was also relieved to see that several of the others looked as nervous as she was.

But where was Renee? In answer to her unspoken question, the tap-tap of high heels echoed from the back of the studio. Mac was looking at his watch impatiently, and he waved to Renee.

"We're down here," he called out.

"Sorry I'm late," Renee said sweetly. She sauntered toward the chairs, and Carrie could tell she was aware of everyone's eyes on her. She had on a tiny miniskirt, with an off-the-shoulder sweater. Very sexy, Carrie thought—the kind of thing she herself would never have the guts to wear.

Mac gave her a brief smile.

"Ok, kids, let me make one point right now. We're running on a tight schedule here. Time is of the essence, and we have to be prompt. So when I say nine o'clock, I mean nine o'clock, and not ten after."

He said it kindly, but it was a reprimand nonetheless. Carrie would have just died if it had been aimed at her. She glanced at Renee to see how she was taking it. Renee simply tossed her long blond hair to the side and looked totally unconcerned.

"We're all going to be working together pretty closely over the next couple of weeks," Mac continued. "So let's spend a few minutes getting to know one another." They went around the circle, and each extra introduced him- or herself. Carrie knew she wouldn't remember each name, but she figured she'd learn them eventually. When they finished, Mac went on.

"I know you're all excited, nervous, and wondering what you'll be doing. Let me start by telling you about this video, and the kind of roles you'll be playing."

All eyes were on him as he described the story that would be played out. Based on a soon-to-be-released record, the video would focus on a boy who had a reputation for being a heartbreaker, a real love-'em-and-leave-'em type. But it was made clear that he didn't deserve the reputation; he only got this image because girls kept chasing him, and he wasn't interested in just any girl. He was only interested in one special girl, but she ignored him because of his reputation.

"There are four scenes," Mac said. "The first scene is set in a typical high-school classroom. The boy enters, and all the girls, except one, turn to look at him. Two of the girls try to take his arms, but he brushes them aside. He approaches the one special girl, but she moves away from him. In the next scene, you will all be in a video game arcade. The boy enters, and the same business goes on. The third scene is set in a restaurant, where you will all be customers, and the final scene is set in a disco, where the girls leave their dancing partners to gather around the boy."

"Does he ever get together with that special girl?" a pretty redheaded girl asked.

Mac grinned. "Absolutely. I like a happy ending!"

"What are the other boys doing all this time?" Mark Clinton asked.

"Looking hostile," Mac said, "and trying to get their girls back. When we have our first run-through on Monday, I'll be showing each of you your specific roles and movements. Any questions so far?"

Carrie looked around the room. She had a pretty good suspicion that they were all wondering the same thing. But Mac hadn't even mentioned the name that was on everyone's mind. And obviously, no one wanted to be the first to ask about him. As if he was reading their minds, Mac smiled and said, "About Michael Jackson—"

Everyone looked at him expectantly. He paused, as if he was almost at a loss for words. Given the subject, Carrie could understand. How could anyone describe the sensation of Michael Jackson?

"I know you're all very excited about meeting and working with Michael Jackson," Mac said. "I don't need to tell you he's the most dazzling, brilliant performer on the music scene. He's a record industry phenomenon. But I think you'll all find him to be a very pleasant, polite young man, not at all pretentious or conceited. Michael's a professional, which means he'll be giving his all to this video. I expect the same of all of you."

One of the extras—Carrie thought her name might be Brenda—said, "I read in a magazine that he's very shy."

Mac looked thoughtful. "I can't answer that," he said finally. "Remember that you can't always believe everything you read in fan magazines. But I've worked with a lot of so-called celebrities, and I'll tell you this: the nicest thing you can do for them is to respect their privacy. Privacy is important to everyone, but it's particularly important for people who are in the limelight so much of the time."

He paused again and then looked at them all very seriously.

"You may find this hard to believe, but in my business, I've seen that being a superstar is not the easiest role in the world. There are a lot of pressures involved, a lot of unique problems. It's not always the happiest position to be in."

Carrie found this a little hard to believe. After all, who wouldn't want to be gorgeous, talented, rich, famous, and adored by millions? But she made a promise to herself to follow Mac's advice and not gush over the superstar. It wouldn't be easy, though.

"Other questions?" Mac asked.

Renee raised a hand languidly. "Who's the special girl? The one who gets the boy?"

"I'm glad you asked that," Mac said. "This is Nina Taylor."

A beautiful young woman who had introduced herself briefly earlier rose from her chair. Carrie had noticed her—she seemed more confident than the others there.

"Nina is a young actress who has appeared in several films and TV shows," Mac said.

The tall, slender brunette smiled widely. "My appearances have been very brief," she said. "This is the biggest part I've ever had." The appreciative look she gave Mac indicated that she was very grateful.

Mac went on to describe their schedule. They'd have a week of rehearsals, beginning on Monday. Then there would be a week of filming.

"Wow," exclaimed an extra, "how long is this video going to be?"

Mac laughed. "The actual video will only last about four minutes and thirty seconds. But believe me, it'll take a lot longer to film."

Mac talked about what they could expect

to do, what the sets would be like, costumes, and a lot of other details.

"Now," he said, "I've got a special treat for you. I am now going to play the song this video is based on. As I mentioned before, the record hasn't been released yet. You kids are the first to hear it."

He put a cassette on a small tape player and punched a button. The room was incredibly silent as the extras sat on the edge of their seats and listened intently.

The song began with a solo guitar that merged with a rocking, rhythmic percussion. Then that immediately recognizable, unforgettable voice came on.

Carrie closed her eyes and allowed herself to be swept away by this tale of misunderstanding and unrequited love. The song had a great beat—Carrie felt as if she could jump up and dance to it. But there was more to it than that. The lyrics were poignant and sensitive—you could hear joy, sadness, hurt, hope. As she listened, Carrie knew she was hearing one of the great rock 'n' roll songs of all time.

When the record was over, there was a silence. This was followed by a spontaneous burst of applause. Mac joined them.

"I wish I could take the credit for this, but

I can't," he said. "I can assure you, though, that we'll be creating a video that will meet the standards of this song. While your roles may sound minor, you'll all be playing a very important part in this production. I can guarantee you that you're in for two weeks of very hard work—but when this video hits the airwaves, I can also guarantee you that your efforts will have been very worthwhile."

His words had the effect of a successful pep talk. Carrie felt a real sense of excitement. She looked around, and she could see that everyone else's expression was reflecting the same sense of anticipation. She felt incredibly lucky to be a part of all this.

Mac passed out some forms they all had to fill out and have signed by their parents. Carrie bent over the form and began writing her name and address.

"Excited?"

Carrie looked up into Joe's warm brown eyes. "Oh, I am," she said. "This has got to be the most exciting thing that's ever happened to me." She hoped she didn't sound like a child. After all, Joe was a senior.

He did smile, but she could tell he wasn't laughing at her.

"I'm excited, too," he confided. "Mac's

supposed to be a terrific director, and with Michael Jackson, you know it's going to be a fantastic video." He pulled up a chair by her.

"Like Mac said, we're all going to be working pretty closely together the next couple of weeks. Maybe we should get to know each other better."

Was he getting at what Carrie thought he was getting at?

"I'd like that," she said carefully.

A wide smile broke out on his face. "I was wondering if maybe you'd like to go out Saturday night?" he asked. "I can get tickets for a rock concert, I think."

For a second Carrie couldn't respond, and the smile left Joe's face. "You've probably already got plans," he started to say.

"Oh, no," Carrie said hastily. "I'd like to go out with you."

The smile returned to his face. "Great," he said. He wrote down Carrie's address and looked at his watch.

"I've got to run," he said. "I'll pick you up Saturday night at eight, OK?"

Carrie sat there in a total daze. What a day! Not only was she working in a music video, a Michael Jackson video, she had just met a really nice, great-looking guy, a professional singer, who seemed interested in her! She couldn't wait to get home and call Susan and Amy. . . .

Thinking about getting home made her look around for Renee. She saw her sitting alone, filling out the form.

"Renee, how are you getting home?"

Renee looked at her as if she had just asked an incredibly stupid question. "Driving, of course," she said. "I got my own car when I turned sixteen last month."

Carrie waited to see if Renee would offer her a ride.

"I suppose you want a ride," Renee said finally. Her offer was so ungracious that Carrie was tempted to refuse. But even riding with Renee would be better than waiting for a bus.

"Thanks," said Carrie. "I'll get my purse and be right with you." She stopped to say goodbye to Mac and to thank him again for this opportunity. Then she joined Renee, and they left the studio and got into Renee's car.

"Who was that cute guy you were talking to?" Renee asked.

"His name's Joe," Carrie said. She couldn't resist adding, "He asked me out for this weekend."

"That's nice," Renee said in a disinterested voice. There was silence.

"I noticed several other cute guys there," Carrie said at last. "That Mark Clinton's very good-looking."

"Mmm, I suppose so." Again, Renee didn't sound very interested. Carrie was surprised. Renee usually reacted to good-looking guys the same way a child responded to candy.

Renee seemed to read her mind. "I'm not interested in any extras," she said in a disdainful voice. "I have bigger plans, if you know what I mean."

Carrie didn't. "Huh?"

Renee laughed. "You'll see what I mean."

As they drove in silence, Carrie puzzled over Renee's words. What could she be talking about? A thought suddenly occurred to her. No—that was impossible. Surely Renee couldn't be planning to go after Michael Jackson!

Chapter Five

The phone was ringing as she walked in the house.

"Tell, tell, tell!" It was Amy, but Carrie knew Susan was there, too—she could hear her in the background, pleading, "What's she saying?"

"It was *neat*," Carrie said, and she began to tell her about the video. Then she heard Susan wrestle the phone away from Amy.

"Was *he* there?" she asked breathlessly.

Carrie smiled to herself. "Who?" she asked innocently.

"Carrie!"

She laughed. "No, Michael Jackson wasn't there, not today. But he *will* be. And let me tell you about Joe—"

"Joe? Who's Joe?" Carrie proceeded to describe him. "He's so cute," she said as she visualized him. "Great brown eyes, curly hair that falls down onto his forehead—"

"He sounds like Michael Jackson," Susan interrupted. Carrie thought for a minute.

"Maybe—yeah, he does look a little bit like him," she said.

"Is he another extra in the video?"

"More than that," Carrie replied. "He's a back-up singer, a professional one. And he's worked with some really big stars—"

"Wow," Susan said.

"And he asked me out!" Carrie finished triumphantly.

"Carrie, that's fantastic!" Susan shrieked. Now Carrie could hear Amy yelling, "What did she say?" And Carrie waited while Susan reported the news. Then Amy took the phone.

"By the way," Amy then asked in a slightly more subdued tone, "did you happen to talk to Renee? I mean, did she say anything more about Barry? Not that I'm worried . . ."

Carrie reported her peculiar conversation with Renee on the way home from the studio. "She says she has bigger plans," she concluded.

"You don't think that means she's actually going to go after Michael Jackson?!"

"I don't know," Carrie replied. "But it sure sounds that way."

"Gosh," Amy said. She sounded half incredulous, half impressed. "I know Renee's conceited and she thinks she can get any guy in the world, but—Michael Jackson?"

Carrie heard the front door open. "Mom's home," she said. "I'd better go. I'll talk to you later."

Her mother was just as anxious as Amy and Susan to hear all about Carrie's day. As they prepared dinner together in the kitchen, Carrie gave her a detailed, blow-by-blow report, and her mother responded with enthusiasm. But when Carrie got to the part about her upcoming date with Joe, she saw that her mother's smile seemed to fade.

"I don't know, Carrie," she said with a slight frown. "If he's a professional singer. . . . Well, I've read about these rock 'n' roll types. Some of them are pretty wild—"

"I don't think Joe's like that," Carrie said. "He looks pretty straight to me. And he says he's saving all his recording money for college. Honestly, Mom, wait till you meet him."

"OK, honey," her mother said, but there

was still some doubt on her face. Carrie decided not to mention right then that they might be going to a rock concert. Better to let her mother meet Joe first. She'd see right away that he wasn't one of those weird punk rockers.

When Saturday evening finally arrived, Carrie was still going through her usual anxieties over what to wear. Assorted shirts, skirts, and jeans were strewn all over her bed, and she glared at them all in dismay. *Nothing* looked right.

"Mom!" she called out in desperation. "Help!"

Her mother appeared in the doorway, her hands behind her back. "What's the problem?"

"I've got nothing to wear!" Carrie wailed. Her mother glanced at the clothes on the bed and shook her head in amusement.

"Well, I wouldn't say *that*," she said. "However, I had a funny feeling *you* would. Maybe this will help." And she held up a bright turquoise jump suit.

"Mom!" Carrie screamed. "That's gorgeous! It's absolutely perfect!"

Her mother beamed, obviously enjoying Carrie's reaction.

As Carrie started pulling on the outfit, the doorbell rang. She ran to her window and peered out.

"Oh, no!" she moaned desperately. "He's early!"

"Once again, Mom to the rescue," her mother said comfortingly. "I'll entertain him while you make yourself gorgeous."

Carrie frantically searched her jewelry box for the little turquoise stud earrings that would be perfect with the new jump suit. When she was dressed, she surveyed herself in the mirror. The bright outfit seemed to add a nice glow to her skin. And her hair looked like it would stay curly and not turn into frizz. She added a hint of blusher to her cheeks and some pink gloss to her lips.

Not bad, she decided. Maybe she wasn't a raving beauty, but, in all modesty, she had to admit she looked pretty cute. Well, she had kept Joe waiting long enough. Maybe it was good that he was early, she thought as she descended the stairs. This would give her mother a chance to check him out and see for herself that he wasn't some wild and crazy rocker.

And when she finally made her grand entrance, she knew immediately that all was well. Joe was talking, her mother was nodding, and Carrie could read approval all over her mother's face.

"And if I can continue to get recording work while I'm in college, I'll be able to save enough for medical school, too."

"Hi!" Carrie said brightly. "Sorry to keep you waiting."

Joe jumped up from his chair. "I was early," he said. "I wasn't sure how to get here, so I wanted to allow plenty of time." He gave Carrie an admiring look. "You look great!"

"Thanks," Carrie said. "So do you!" It was true, but as soon as the words left her lips, she wanted to take them back. What a dumb thing to say! But Joe actually seemed pleased. And he *did* look great. He had on a pale yellow sweater, the same color sweater Michael Jackson was wearing in her bedroom poster.

"I've got tickets for Van Halen," he said. "I hope you like them."

Carrie gasped. "Van Halen! That's been sold out for weeks! How did you get tickets?"

Joe smiled modestly. "Because of my recording work—well, I've got connections."

"What's a 'Van Halen'?" her mother asked.

"They're a band," Joe explained. "Heavy metal."

"Oh, I see," replied Mrs. Philips, although her expression clearly indicated that she didn't know what he was talking about. Carrie looked at her apprehensively.

"Well," her mother said, "I'm not crazy about the idea of rock concerts. I hear the crowds can get pretty crazy."

"This one should be OK," Joe assured her. "It's indoors, and reserved seating. I'll take good care of Carrie, Mrs. Philips."

Carrie looked at him with admiration. He seemed so mature, the kind of guy who could inspire confidence. And she could tell he was having the right kind of effect on her mother. Her worried look had softened.

"OK, kids," she said. "Just be careful and have a good time."

Joe's car was parked out front, and he held the door open for Carrie. "Welcome to my pride and joy," he said, patting the not-very-new but well-kept car fondly.

"Is this your own car?" Carrie asked.

"Yep," Joe said proudly as he slid behind the driver's seat. "My one major extravagance.

But it's also a necessity. I needed a car to get around to the different recording studios."

"I heard you telling my mother something about saving money for medical school."

Joe nodded, keeping his eyes on the road as he drove.

"Right," he said. "As long as I can remember I've wanted to be a doctor." His voice became quiet. "My father was a doctor, and he always seemed to get so much pleasure from his work. He—he died last year."

Carrie replied softly. "Then we have something in common. My father died when I was just a baby."

They had stopped at a red light. They looked at each other, and an unspoken message of understanding passed between them.

"Anyway," Joe said, "that's one reason why I'm glad to get the recording work, and now this video job. I need the money for college and medical school."

"I know how expensive that can be," Carrie said. "I guess I'm lucky. My parents set up a college trust fund for me when I was born. But I'm hoping to have enough money to go to law school after."

"You're planning to become a lawyer?"

"I think so," Carrie said. "Not the business kind, though. I want to work for a legal-aid society. You know, fight injustice, help people get their civil rights, that sort of thing. I guess that sounds pretty idealistic."

"Not at all," Joe said. "You know, most people think all doctors are rich. But my dad wasn't the kind of doctor who had a fancy office and charged huge fees. Mostly he liked to help really needy people, and if they couldn't pay, well, he'd take care of them, anyway." He paused, then added seriously, "That's the kind of doctor I want to be. I want to help the people who really need help."

Carrie felt a warm sense of appreciation for this boy who seemed to have the same kinds of feelings about people as she did. But one thing puzzled her.

"Didn't you ever consider a career as a singer?" she asked. "I mean, you must be really talented if you can get work as a back-up singer at your age."

Joe grinned. "I guess I'm a pretty good singer," he admitted. "At least, that's what people tell me. Of course, I'm no Michael Jackson, but I've always liked to sing. And recording work certainly pays a lot better than waiting tables or washing cars! But singing is really just a hobby for me. I guess I've always had my heart set on being a doctor. How about you? You said you've been taking dance classes. Have you ever thought about being a dancer?"

Carrie laughed at the thought.

"The classes are just for fun and exercise," she said. "I'm not the performing type! But I think it must be fun to be in show business— all that glamour—"

"It's not so glamorous," Joe said. "From my experience, I can tell you it's a lot of drudgery and hard work. And the pressure can be fierce."

For the rest of the ride, they talked about their interests, compared high schools, and discussed the video. Carrie marveled at how easy it was to talk with Joe. He was such a comfortable person to be with. By the time they arrived at the auditorium, she felt as if she had known him forever.

The concert was fantastic. The band was so loud she and Joe couldn't say a word to each other. Even between the songs, the yelling and applause from the audience made any conversation impossible. But the music was wonderful—steely guitars, frenzied bursts of drumming, and a flashy, sexy lead singer who had all the girls in the crowd screaming.

It was during the first encore that Carrie felt Joe's hand on her own. She relaxed her hand, letting his fingers intertwine with hers. It seemed so natural, it felt so—right, she thought,

After the concert, still holding hands, they moved out with the crowd and strolled around the building to the parking lot on the side.

"Look," Joe said, pointing toward the side of the auditorium. Carrie saw about a hundred kids, maybe more, gathered in front of a side door and screaming for the band members by name.

"I hope the band doesn't have to come out that way," Joe said. "They might not get out alive."

Carrie stared at the crowd. "It must be exciting, though, to have so many fans," she said. "Just to know that all those people adore you."

Joe laughed. "I'll bet it's not so exciting when the fans chase them to their cars, rip their clothes, and pull their hair!"

Carrie's eyes widened. "Would they really do that?"

Joe nodded. "I've seen some fans go totally berserk. I guess it's the price of fame. Hey, are you hungry?"

Since she'd been too nervous before their date to eat any dinner, Carrie wasn't surprised to find herself aware of an empty feeling in her stomach. "Starving," she admitted.

They drove to a popular pizza place, and Joe ordered them a pizza with everything. As they ate, they talked about some of the other people working on the video.

"That Mark Clinton seems like a nice guy," Carrie commented.

"Yeah, I talked to him for a while the other day," Joe said. A long strand of cheese refused to become separated from the bite he had just taken, and it wrapped itself on the bottom of his chin. He had to use his fingers to break it off, and he looked sort of embarrassed.

Carrie smiled sympathetically. That was the kind of thing that always happened to her.

"Anyway," Joe continued, "I think he's got ambitions. He sees this video as the beginning of a big career." He sighed. "I hope the poor guy knows what he's in for."

"What do you mean?"

Joe looked thoughtful. "In my work, just being on the fringes of show business, I've seen a lot of people get burned. Not that many actually make it to the top." He paused, as if he were trying to decide whether or not he would say what he wanted to say. Carrie smiled encouragingly.

"You know," Joe said slowly, "when I first started doing recording work, I *did* think, maybe, I might want to make a career of it. But when I saw what it did to people—the pressures, all that—well, I decided I just wasn't suited for it."

"Why?" Carrie asked curiously. Joe seemed like such a confident person. She couldn't imagine him not being able to handle anything.

"I'm kind of a private person," Joe admitted. "I know I wouldn't like all that attention. Besides, I'm not that great a singer. I probably couldn't make it even if I wanted to. I'm an OK singer—but I'm not in the star category."

"I'll bet you're just being modest," Carrie said.

Joe grinned. "I'm not modest. I know I'll be a great doctor! How about you? Why do you want to be a lawyer?"

"I get so angry when I see injustice," she said passionately. "I remember once, when I was a kid, everyone was picking on this girl at school because they thought she was stealing stuff from other kids' desks. I knew she wasn't doing it. At first I was too shy to defend her. But finally, I did—and I felt so good about it."

And then it was her turn to reveal something personal about herself. "I've always been pretty shy," she admitted. "To be honest, the thought of standing up and talking in a courtroom terrifies me. But I guess I'll get over that."

"I think if you want something bad enough, you do what you have to do to get it," Joe said. "I'll bet you'll be a great lawyer." The way he said it, Carrie could almost believe it.

Later that evening, as they stood on her doorstep, there was an awkward moment.

"I had a wonderful time," Carrie said.

"Me, too," Joe replied.

There was a silence. Would he kiss her good night? She looked into his eyes and smiled. Was he thinking about the same thing?

He put his hands on her shoulders, pulled her gently toward him, and kissed her lightly.

"I'll see you at the studio on Monday," he whispered.

Carrie floated into the house, closed the door, and then leaned against it dreamily. All that nervousness she had felt earlier had evaporated during the evening. She couldn't remember ever feeling so comfortable with a boy. She was feeling something else, too, something she had never felt before. So much was happening so fast—was this the beginning of something? *I really like that boy,* she thought, and a thrill went through her. *Now hold on,* she warned herself. *Don't get carried away. It was only a first date. It was just one kiss.*

But she had a pretty good feeling it wouldn't be their last.

Chapter Six

The memory of that kiss and the warmth of his hand in hers lasted right through to Monday morning as Carrie entered Studio 7B. She wondered how she'd feel when she saw Joe. Would it be awkward?

She didn't have long to worry. Joe was already there, and the light in his eyes when he saw Carrie assured her that he remembered the kiss, too.

"Hi," he said, smiling warmly. "Ready for the run-through?"

"I hope so," Carrie replied, returning his smile. "What *is* a run-through, anyway?"

"Nothing to worry about," he assured her. "I think Mac's just planning to have us walk through the different sequences. The sets aren't up yet, so we'll probably just be working right here."

The other extras were drifting in, and Carrie was glad to see that Renee was on time. She had on supertight, cropped jeans and a tank top that didn't leave much to the imagination. She strolled over to Carrie and Joe.

"Hi," she murmured languidly. "What are we doing today, anyway?" Again Joe explained the purpose of a run-through. Mark Clinton overheard and joined them to listen. When Joe finished, Renee gave a yawn that suggested boredom and disappointment.

"So I guess Michael Jackson won't be showing up today," she said.

"Probably not," Joe replied.

Mark was looking at Renee with obvious interest. "I'm Mark Clinton," he said. "I don't think I caught your name the other day."

Renee gave him the briefest possible acknowledgment. "Renee," she said shortly and walked away.

Poor Mark, Carrie thought, *I guess he doesn't fit into her "bigger plans."*

"OK, kids, let's gather over here." Mac was calling them from an area of the studio where chairs had been set up in even rows as in a classroom. The extras gathered around him.

"This will give you a rough idea of what the first set will look like," he said. "It will be a typical classroom. Some of you will be sitting at desks, others will be standing around. Right now, I'm going to show each of you where you'll be, and I want you to remember your positions."

He looked over the group, and Carrie glanced around, too. She could tell many of the kids were looking uneasy. She was feeling a little tense herself. This was it—they were really going to work now, and she knew she'd better listen carefully.

"Brenda, over here," Mac said, and a petite brunette moved forward. Mac indicated a seat, and she sat down.

"Should I sit forward or to the side?" Brenda asked uncertainly.

"Don't worry about that yet," Mac said briskly. "Just stay put for now. Mark, I want you leaning against that wall."

He went on calling out names and directing extras to seats or places to stand. One girl, Lauren, misunderstood her direction, and Mac repeated his order in a sharp voice. Lauren looked as if she was about to burst into tears. Mac sighed.

"Look, kids, you'll learn soon enough that I have a tendency to bark," he said with a wry smile. "Don't take it personally. It's just my style, OK?"

Carrie nodded along with the others, but she hoped fervently that she'd never hear Mac's bark directed at her.

Mac pointed her toward a chair, and Carrie sat down. She saw Joe and Mark leaning against a wall. All the extras who were in the chairs were sitting very stiffly and looking unnatural. Mac stood in front of them and surveyed the scene.

"OK," he said. "This is where you'll be in the first scene as the video begins. When Michael enters, some of you will be leaving your seats, others will be simply changing positions to look at him. I'll be taking Michael's part for today."

He paused and grinned impishly.

"I'll just be *walking* through his part, not dancing. I wouldn't dare try to do what Michael's planning for this sequence! I'm afraid my body isn't capable of doing what Michael's can do."

Some of the extras chuckled at the

thought of the slightly pudgy, balding Mac dancing like Michael Jackson.

"But," Mac continued, "just to put myself in the proper frame of mind—" He reached into his back pocket, pulled out a sequined white glove, and carefully slipped it over his right hand. Now everyone was laughing as Mac solemnly struck a dance pose, his gloved right hand held high.

Carrie felt herself begin to relax, and she suspected that was Mac's intent—to get all the extras to loosen up and relax and be natural.

Just then Nina came running in. Carrie had been wondering where the pretty actress was.

"Sorry to be late," she called out to the extras, and then she had a hurried, whispered conversation with Mac. He didn't seem disturbed by her tardiness, and he directed her to the empty seat next to Carrie.

Nina slipped into the seat and smiled at Carrie. She seemed to be out of breath.

"I've been rehearsing with Michael on another set," she told her.

Carrie's eyes widened. "Wow," she exclaimed, "that must be an experience."

Nina rolled her eyes. "No kidding," she said. "Believe me, it's not easy trying to keep up with Michael. I've studied dance for years, but I've never seen anyone who can move like he can."

Just from having seen Michael dance in videos, Carrie could believe it.

Mac began giving each of them individual, specific instructions. Carrie was relieved to learn that her part in this sequence wasn't too big. All she had to do was to lean sideways in her chair and gaze wistfully at Michael—or in this case, Mac. She hoped she'd be able to make the right expression. She had a feeling it wouldn't be too difficult when the real Michael Jackson was standing there!

She felt a little twinge of envy when she heard Renee get her instructions.

"When Michael comes in," Mac was saying, "he'll stop here. Then, Renee, you'll get up from your seat and stroll over to him. Can you do a sort of sexy walk?"

Carrie almost laughed out loud when she heard that question. That was the only way Renee *could* walk!

"Then you'll take his arm," Mac continued, still talking to Renee. "Lauren will take his other arm. Michael will do a spin of some sort, lightly pushing both of you away, and he'll move toward Nina. Nina, you'll twist around in your seat so that your back is to him."

Nina nodded to indicate that she understood. Then she grinned at Carrie. "I wonder how realistic this is going to look," she whispered. "After all, what girl in her right mind would turn her back on Michael Jackson!"

"Do you all understand your instructions?" Mac called out to the group. The chorus of affirmative replies didn't sound too confident, but Mac didn't seem concerned.

"I'm not expecting perfection," Mac said. "This is our first run-through. Now, stretch your imaginations to their limits and pretend I'm Michael Jackson entering here."

Everyone did what they were supposed to do, and they all looked pretty awkward to Carrie, but Mac didn't seem too displeased when they finished walking through the sequence.

"Not bad, not bad," he said encouragingly. "Let's go through it again."

Carrie could see some improvement this time. When they finished, Mac looked at them with approval.

"Now you're getting the general idea," he said.

"How come we're not doing this to the music?" an extra asked.

"Tomorrow we'll start working with the record," Mac said. "Today, I want you all to concentrate on the visual aspect. If we had the music playing now, it would just make it all seem more confusing. Now, we're going to run through the second sequence." He called to a couple of men, who began pushing the chairs away.

"In this sequence," Mac explained, "the set will look like a video game arcade. There will be video games set up around the perimeter of the set. Some of you will be playing them, others will be standing around and watching."

Again Mac called each extra individually and showed him or her where to stand and what to pretend to be doing. Carrie would be playing a game, while Mark and another extra stood on either side of her, watching. Mac told her that when Michael came in, she should turn away from the game, place a hand over her heart, and look as if she were about to swoon. Carrie felt a little silly doing this, but at least she wasn't one of the girls who had to fall on the floor in a dead faint!

As they walked through the scene, Carrie

kept one eye on Joe to see what he'd be doing. Mac was playing Michael's role again, and when he entered, Joe walked toward him in a swaggering way. When directly in front of Mac, he had to stop and sneer.

He did it very well, and Carrie was impressed. Joe looked like he was really angry.

They walked through the arcade scene twice. Several times Mac stopped them and barked at a couple of extras who were moving in the wrong directions. But by the time they finished running through the scene the second time, they were all getting used to Mac's manner, and no one looked too upset.

"All right, everyone," Mac yelled, "we've put in a good morning's work. Let's break for lunch now."

He told them they would only get forty-five minutes, but the studio was providing box lunches right on the set to save time. Carrie picked up her box and looked around to see where she could sit.

"Let's go over there," Joe said from behind her. They moved over to a bench in a corner of the room.

"I had a great time Saturday night," Joe said.

Carrie had just bitten into her sandwich,

and she chewed frantically so she could smile and say, "Me, too."

There was a moment of silence, and then Carrie decided suddenly to ask what her mother had suggested that morning on the way to the studio.

"I was wondering . . ." she began and then paused. Would he think she was being pushy? Well, might as well take a chance.

"Would you like to come over for dinner tonight?" she finished in a rush.

In an instant she was glad she had taken the chance. Joe's face lit up.

"I'd like that," he said. "I'll have to call my mother, but I'm sure it'll be OK."

"Mind if I join you guys?"

Carrie managed to take her eyes off Joe and look up at Nina, standing there with her lunch box in her hands.

"Please do," she said, and Nina pulled up a chair.

"I'm beat," she said as she flopped down. "I still haven't recovered from this morning with Michael."

"He's got incredible energy," Joe said. "I can't wait to see what kind of dancing he's going to do in this video."

"It'll be amazing," Nina said firmly. "The

72

part at the end where I dance with him is the most difficult dancing I've ever done."

"Have you been performing for a long time?" Carrie asked.

Nina gave an exaggerated groan. "I've been *trying* to," she said. "I've been going to auditions and trying out for parts for years—oh gosh, at least since I was sixteen."

Carrie stared at her. Nina didn't look much older than that now!

"How old *are* you?" Carrie asked impulsively, then bit her lip. That wasn't a very polite question to ask! But Nina just laughed.

"I'm twenty-six," she said. "Luckily, I look younger, or I'd never have gotten this part."

"It must be incredibly exciting to work closely with someone like Michael Jackson," Carrie said.

Nina nodded enthusiastically. "It is. He's a marvelous person, as well as a great talent. He's very thoughtful and thoroughly professional. I'm learning so much just watching him."

"Have you ever done a video before?" Joe asked.

Nina shook her head. "No, all I've ever done are 'bits'—you know, walk-ons, as an extra in a couple of made-for-TV movies."

Carrie thought she saw a sad look in the beautiful girl's eyes.

"Once," Nina continued wistfully, "I had a couple of lines in a real movie—but the scene was cut in the editing room." She shrugged lightly. "I guess that's show biz."

"It's a rough business," Joe murmured. "I really admire people who can stick it out. I mean, there are all these people coming down on you, making you feel like a big zero."

Nina nodded in agreement. "This is my first big break," she said, "after ten years." Then she gave a halfhearted laugh. "But I don't know how much good it will do me. I mean, with Michael Jackson on the screen, who's going to notice me?"

The three of them had just finished their lunches when they heard Mac call, "Extras, back on the set!"

Nina, Joe, and Carrie threw out their boxes and walked back to the rehearsal area. Carrie was looking at the new configuration of chairs, set up in facing pairs, when she became aware that the studio had become unnaturally quiet. Turning around, she suddenly realized why everyone was silent.

Standing there, just a few yards away, talking quietly with Mac, was Michael Jackson.

Chapter Seven

He was dressed casually, in a red- and white-striped T-shirt and blue jeans, white socks and loafers. He looked exactly like his pictures—slender and graceful, a curly lock of hair hanging down on his forehead and sunglasses hiding his eyes. He didn't appear to be aware of everyone looking at him. Mac was telling him something, and Michael was nodding.

Carrie remembered what Mac had said about respecting his privacy, and she tried not to stare, but she couldn't help herself. There he was, a living legend, the greatest pop superstar in music today, maybe the greatest ever. She remembered an article about him she had read in a magazine. The writer had called him a "thriller" and reported that the album of the same name had sold more than any other album, ever. The singles from the album, the videos of the singles, the posters—all had sold more than any others in the entire history of rock 'n' roll.

Singer, dancer, ultimate performer—and there he was, live and in person. No wonder the room was completely silent. It was as if they were in the presence of a magical phenomenon. And maybe they were.

Carrie couldn't believe what she saw next, though. Renee left the group and walked over to Mac and Michael. She seemed to be saying something to them, but then, a second later, she was walking away. Mac and Michael talked for a few more minutes, and then Michael left the studio.

Mac came back to the extras. "OK, kids, let's run through the next scene. This is a fast-food restaurant. Brenda, would you sit here, please."

Carrie found herself placed in a seat that Mac explained would be a restaurant booth. She was still in a daze, unable to believe that she had just seen Michael Jackson. Suddenly she realized that Renee was being seated in the chair across from her, and for once she was glad to see her.

"Renee, what did you say to him?" she asked eagerly. Renee was looking very pleased with herself. She tossed her head so her long hair flipped over her shoulder.

"I introduced myself," she said smugly, "while the rest of you were staring and gawking like groupies."

Carrie contained her annoyance at being referred to as a groupie, but she forced herself to look pleasant. She wanted to hear the whole story. "But what did you actually say?"

Renee looked blasé. "I said, 'Hi, Michael, I'm Renee Mitchell.' That's all."

"And what did *he* say?" Carrie asked eagerly.

Renee tossed her head again. "He was very nice."

"But what did he actually *say*?" Carrie persisted.

Renee looked annoyed, but finally she admitted that all Michael actually had said was hello. "But he gave me a *very* meaningful look," Renee hastened to add. "I mean, I could tell from the way he looked at me that . . . well"—she smiled in a phony humble way— "he admired me."

Carrie shook her head and gave Renee her own version of a "meaningful" look.

"Oh, knock it off, Renee," she said. "He was probably just being polite."

The phony expression seemed to dissolve from her face and was replaced by one of peculiar intensity. "Carrie," Renee whispered, "I've got to get him to notice me, to single me out from the others."

Carrie stared at her. "Renee, practically every girl in the world has a crush on Michael Jackson. He's everyone's fantasy. You're not serious about this, are you?"

Renee looked impatient. "Hey, I'm not crazy," she said. "I'm not expecting him to fall madly in love with me. I just want him to notice me. Of course," she added slyly, "I wouldn't mind if he asked me out."

Carrie raised her eyebrows.

"Renee, be realistic," she said. "Don't you read the magazines? He's in a whole different social world. He dates girls like Brooke Shields."

Renee waved her hand as if to brush that comment aside. "That's just publicity. They were probably fixed up by their press agents. I'll bet there's nothing at all between them."

Carrie looked doubtful. "I wouldn't count

on that," she said. "From everything I've read about Michael Jackson, he doesn't seem to be the kind of person who would go out with a girl just for publicity. I'll bet he really likes her."

Renee couldn't respond to that because Mac was calling for everyone's attention. All Carrie had to do in this scene was lean back in her chair and look infatuated.

It was the next scene that had her a little apprehensive. This was the disco scene, the scene where Michael and Nina would finally get together. All the extras would be dancing in the scene. Then Michael would come in, and they'd all freeze. He and Nina would look at each other, then come together and dance.

Mac patiently explained to them all that he wasn't expecting professional dancing.

"I just want you to be dancing like you normally would at a dance or a disco," he explained. "Nothing fancy, no running around on the floor. Try to stay in one place and simply move to the rhythm of the music. Michael, of course, and Nina will be providing the flashy stuff. Again, I don't want to use the music yet, so you won't actually dance today. I just want to position you so you'll see where you'll be dancing."

Carrie felt some temporary relief knowing she wouldn't actually have to dance yet. Even though she'd been to school dances, and no one had ever actually laughed at her dancing, she worried that she might look gawky compared with the other kids. But maybe her dance classes would pay off, and she might not look so bad after all.

Mac started calling out names and pairing the extras as couples for the disco scene.

"Renee, I want you over here with Mark." Mark looked pleased, but Renee immediately applied her I'm-so-bored-with-all-this look as she sauntered across the floor to join him.

"Carrie, you'll be over here with Joe."

Carrie felt a rush of happiness, followed immediately by a sense of panic—what would he think of her dancing? But her concern began to fade when she saw the obvious pleasure on his face.

"Now this is what I call perfect casting," he said as she joined him.

All they had to do was stand there while Mac showed them how Michael would enter. He explained that once Michael and Nina came together and started dancing, they would slowly move back beyond camera range.

"OK, kids, that's it for today," Mac finally

said. "Tomorrow we'll begin working intensively with the music. By Friday, the sets will be up. You've all put in a good day's work, and I'll see you at nine in the morning."

Joe dashed off to call his mother and returned a few minutes later to report that all was well and he could go home with Carrie for dinner.

As they walked to the car, Joe asked Carrie if she had recovered.

Carrie was puzzled. "I didn't think the day was too exhausting—" she began.

Joe grinned mischievously. "I mean, have you recovered from seeing Michael Jackson in person?"

Carrie felt like blushing. Had she really been gaping like a groupie? Joe laughed as he held the car door open for her. "Everyone looked stunned," he said. "It's a natural response. When you see famous people in real life, it's always a little overwhelming. It's like you can't believe they really exist."

He told her that once when he was working in a recording studio, Linda Ronstadt walked right past him. "I must have looked like an idiot standing there with my mouth open," he said.

"What did *she* do?" Carrie asked.

"Nothing," Joe replied and grinned. "I guess people like that are used to weird reactions."

"I wonder what it feels like to be so recognizable."

"Uncomfortable, I'd guess," Joe said. "Being stared at all the time."

"But it would make a person feel awfully important," Carrie said. "And that could be terrific."

"Maybe," Joe said, but his voice was doubtful. He sounded as if he didn't think that it would be terrific at all. "I'd always wonder if people liked me for myself or because I was a star," he added.

When they arrived home, Carrie was surprised to find her mother already there.

"I was supposed to have a meeting, but it was canceled," Mrs. Philips said after greeting them. "So I decided to come straight home and get to work on something extraspecial for dinner."

The aroma from the kitchen made Joe wrinkle his nose appreciatively. "Whatever it is, it smells wonderful," he said.

Carrie's mother smiled. "It's lasagna," she said. "I hope you like it."

Joe put a hand over his heart and pretended that he was about to faint. "My absolute favorite food in the world!"

Carrie and her mother exchanged glances, and Carrie could tell that her mother was liking Joe more and more.

Dinner was great fun. Joe entertained them both with stories about his experiences in the recording world. He told them about a recording session he had had with one particularly famous rock star.

"A bunch of girls had chased him from his car to the door of the building," he said. "And this poor guy was really scared! He thought if they caught him, they might tear him apart." He chuckled at the memory.

"Anyway," he continued, "when the session was over, he looked out the window, and those girls were still there, waiting for him. He had on this really bright purple jacket. So he asked me if I'd trade coats with him. I had on a plain denim jacket. We were about the same height, and I pushed the collar up to cover part of my face and put on sunglasses. Then I went out first, and as the girls started chasing me, he ran out to his car."

Carrie and her mother were both laughing.

"Weren't you scared of what might happen if they caught you?" Mrs. Philips asked.

"You'd better believe it," Joe replied. "I was shaking!"

"What did happen?" Carrie asked.

Joe grinned ruefully. "When I made sure there was some distance between us, I stopped, turned around, took off the sunglasses, and just stood there. When they realized they'd been had, they ran off to look for their real target. But by then, he had been long gone."

"What a crazy business," Mrs. Philips commented.

Joe nodded. "Some people love it, though. When I first started working, it seemed very glamorous and exciting. Now I think it would be much more exciting to deliver a baby."

"Still," Carrie said, "some parts of the business must be fun."

"Oh, sure," Joe agreed. "When I hear a record I've worked on after it's mixed and released, I always feel proud to know that I was a part of it. Especially if the record hits the charts!"

"Have you ever performed live?" Carrie's mother asked.

Joe nodded. "A couple of times. I was

asked to fill in as a back-up singer for a couple of touring bands in rock concerts."

"What was that like?" Carrie asked.

"Actually, it was kind of fun," Joe admitted. "I've never thought of myself as a performer, but there *is* something exciting about hearing the screams and the applause."

After dinner Mrs. Philips shooed them both out of the kitchen.

"I'll do the dishes tonight, Carrie," she said, giving her daughter a knowing look. "You go entertain your guest."

"Thanks, Mom!"

Joe and Carrie settled themselves in the den. It was the coziest room in the house—small, with a soft rug and two fat overstuffed loveseats. Joe sat down on one of them. Carrie debated for a second—and then sat down next to him.

"What other groups have you performed with?" she asked.

Joe grinned. "For someone who's not interested in a career in show business, you're awfully curious about it!"

Carrie grew thoughtful. "I guess it all just seems so glamorous and romantic to me. Much as I like the idea of becoming a lawyer, compared to acting or dancing or singing, law seems sort of, well, stodgy and dull."

Joe shook his head. "Not if you're planning to go into the kind of law you told me about," he argued. "I think the idea of defending people's rights sounds pretty exciting."

"I know," Carrie said. "But there's something about getting up in front of an audience . . ." She hesitated before going on. Would Joe understand what she was about to tell him? Should she take the risk? Somehow, it seemed like the right thing to do.

She told him about trying out for cheerleading and how her two best friends were chosen and she wasn't. "I felt rejected," she confessed. "As if Amy and Susan were special, and I was just ordinary. But then, when I was picked to be in the video, *I* felt special." She glanced sideways at Joe to see his reaction.

"I know what you mean," he said. "When I didn't make the football team at school last year, I felt just awful. I guess everybody has to find his or her own unique way to feel special."

He paused, then said slowly, "You know, Carrie, when I'm around all those flashy music people, I feel dull and ordinary. I—I always hoped I'd meet someone who could see me as someone special, just the way I am."

Carrie's heart was full. "Oh, Joe," she said, "I know exactly what you mean." She didn't know what to say next. She got up. "How about some music?"

"Sure," Joe said and followed her to the rack of albums next to the stereo. As they flipped through some records, he pulled one out. "Hey, here's one I sang on!" he exclaimed.

Carrie looked over his shoulder. "That's one of my favorites!" She took it from him and put it on the turntable. As the music started, she turned to him. "How about singing along and letting me hear a live performance?"

Joe grinned. "Why not?" He joined in on the back-up part. Carrie sat down and looked up at him. She was entranced. He was really good! His voice was crystal clear, strong, and vibrant. When he finished, she clapped her hands. "Joe, you're a terrific singer!"

Joe looked a little embarrassed. "I think *adequate* is a better word."

"You're a lot more than 'adequate,' " Carrie said. "You're special." Then she bit her lower lip. Had she said too much? she wondered.

Joe was looking at her intently. "And I think *you're* special."

They were very still, just looking at each other. It was a magic moment.

Joe crossed to her and they kissed—more than once.

"I hate to say this," Joe murmured at last, "but it's getting late, and I guess I'd better get going."

Carrie walked him to the door.

"It's been a wonderful evening," Joe said.

"For me, too," Carrie replied.

"I haven't even thanked your mother," he said suddenly.

"I think she's gone to bed," Carrie said. "I'll thank her for you."

They stood there silently, and Carrie knew that Joe was just as reluctant to leave as she was to let him go. Finally they kissed again and said their goodbyes.

Later that night, as she lay in bed, Carrie couldn't stop thinking about him. He was so wonderful! And talented—despite his modesty. He made her feel special. She wondered if she made him feel the same way.

Her eye was caught by the Michael Jackson poster on the wall. Joe was really a good singer, too, she thought. She wondered if she could make him realize just how talented he was. It would be a shame to waste such talent. . . .

And as she drifted off to sleep, still looking at the poster, Michael's face was replaced by Joe's.

Chapter Eight

Coming home on Wednesday afternoon, Carrie felt as if she had been riding a nonstop merry-go-round for the past few days. She couldn't believe rehearsals had been going on for just three days—it felt more like three months. She dragged herself up to her room, collapsed on her bed, closed her eyes, and daydreamed. Susan and Amy would be coming over in an hour, and they'd want every detail of her past days. Her thoughts drifted to the day before. . . .

On Tuesday morning the extras had gone through the classroom scene again. Mr. MacDonald had worked with them on their expressions. "Girls, I know it's not easy for you to imagine I'm Michael Jackson," he said, "but *try*. And when I enter, I want you to give me looks of total rapture. Now let me see you act!"

Carrie concentrated on an image of Michael's face and gave Mac a look that she hoped said "I adore you." Mac surveyed the girls, and he didn't look very pleased.

"Brenda," he said, "you look more like a sick cow than a girl with a crush." He punctuated this with a pleading half smile that took some of the sting out of his words.

"And, Carrie," he said, "your expression is too exaggerated, too artificial. I want something more natural. If thinking about Michael doesn't help, think about someone you really *do* have a crush on."

Automatically, without even thinking, Carrie glanced at Joe leaning against a wall.

"That's it!" Mac said. "Hold on to that expression."

Carrie almost burst out laughing. She hadn't even been *trying* to look infatuated!

When Mac was finally pleased, he told them they'd now go through the scene with music. "This has to be timed perfectly, so prepare yourselves—we'll be going through this over and over till we get it absolutely right."

By the fourth time Mac hit the start button on the tape player, Carrie knew the entire first thirty seconds of the song by heart. Everyone started looking tired, and Mac was getting impatient.

"Lauren, you're not moving quickly enough!" he barked. "You have to move in front of Mark here and take my arm before I get to this point. Now, we'll do it again, and this time get it right!"

Poor Lauren looked terribly flustered, and this time she moved too quickly. She bumped smack into Mark, tripped, and fell.

Everyone froze, except Joe. He immediately went to Lauren and bent down.

"Are you OK?" he asked. By then some of the other extras had gathered around, too.

"Stand back and give her some air!" Joe said firmly, waving them away.

Carrie watched from her seat. She was concerned about Lauren, but she also felt a rush of admiration for Joe's take-charge manner. She could see the kind of doctor he'd be someday—caring and confident.

Joe helped Lauren to her feet.

"I'm OK," Lauren assured them all. "Just stunned, I guess. Thanks, Joe."

"That's OK," Joe said briskly. "You'll get my bill in the morning."

Everyone, including Mac, started laughing, and some of the tension of the morning dissipated.

At lunch Carrie sat with Joe, and she complimented him on the way he had helped Lauren. "You were terrific," she said warmly. "You're a natural doctor, coming to the rescue in an emergency."

Joe grinned appreciatively. "I didn't really do anything," he said. "But I have to say, it felt great pretending to be a doctor! Hey, guess what? This friend of my father's called yesterday, and he says there's a possibility of a part-time orderly job at his hospital."

"Terrific!" Carrie said, but then she frowned. "You'll still be able to work on the video, won't you?"

"Oh, sure," Joe assured her. "The job doesn't start till next month. And I don't even know if I'll get it, anyway. I have to interview."

"I'll bet you get it," Carrie said confidently.

Joe smiled. "You make me feel so good," he said warmly.

In the afternoon they worked on the arcade sequence. By then they were more accustomed to working with the music, and this scene progressed more smoothly than the first one. At one point Mac directed some comments to Joe.

"The camera will be on you several times in this scene," he said. "And you'll need to lip-synch the part that goes 'I'm only looking for you, girl.' Practice that, OK?"

After the rehearsal Joe asked Carrie to stay with him a few minutes to practice the lip-synching.

"This isn't as easy as it looks," he said. "It can look really phony if my lips and the words aren't perfectly synchronized."

Carrie saw what he meant. He practiced with the tape in front of a mirror.

"Look what happens if you miss a word," Joe said. He rewound the tape and started lip-synching again—only this time he started too late. He looked so silly mouthing the wrong words that they both cracked up. The situation wasn't all that funny, but they were both so punchy from the long day that they couldn't stop laughing.

Wednesday had been another long day. In the morning they'd worked on the restaurant scene. Again they had had to go through it over and over before Mac was satisfied.

After lunch they had worked on the most difficult scene—the one set in the disco.

Mac introduced them all to a tall, very slender young man with an intense expression. "This is Jeff Drummond," he said. "He's my assistant director and a choreographer. He'll be observing your dancing and offering a few pointers. Again let me assure you, I just want you all to dance naturally. Jeff is just going to pick out a couple of extras for a special step or two."

They got into their positions, and Mac started the music. Carrie faced Joe, and she began to dance, a little stiffly at first.

But Joe looked completely relaxed, and Carrie was impressed with the way his whole body just seemed to flow with the rhythm of the song. Soon she was able to relax and dance comfortably.

Mr. Drummond approached them.

"I'd like you two to try something," he said. "Watch this." He did a little side step with a slight hop and whirled around. Then he looked at Carrie. "Can you do that?"

It was sort of like one of the steps she had learned in Mrs. Haines's class, and Carrie was pleased to find she could do it easily.

"Fine," the assistant director said and turned to Joe.

"Now let me see you do it."

Joe executed the step precisely. He not only did it correctly, he did it with style. Carrie drew in her breath sharply. When he did the spin, it looked like a real Michael Jackson spin.

"Excellent!" Jeff Drummond said, and he showed them where to incorporate the step in their dancing.

"Joe, you're a wonderful dancer!" Carrie told him later as they were leaving. Joe shrugged and waved the compliment aside.

"Really, you are!" Carrie insisted. "You almost looked like Michael Jackson! You know, I'll bet if you took lessons and practiced—"

"I could be the world's first dancing doctor," Joe finished. As they walked to his car in the studio parking lot, Joe suddenly said, "Look." Carrie turned and saw a group of people walking toward some limousines. In the middle of the group, almost hidden by them, was Michael Jackson.

Carrie only got a quick glimpse of a red leather jacket before the group got into the limousines.

"Who are all those people?" Carrie asked. Joe made a gesture that indicated he wasn't sure.

"I don't know. Press agents, managers, guards, people like that, I guess. He's always surrounded by people." The way he said it, he almost sounded as if he felt sorry for the star.

Now it was late Wednesday afternoon, and Carrie was lying on her bed, still daydreaming about how fantastic Joe had looked when he was dancing. Her dreaming was suddenly cut off by the ringing of the doorbell.

Amy and Susan listened eagerly to Carrie's recital of rehearsal events. They were a perfect audience, oohing and ahhing and interrupting only to say "wow!"

"You've got to meet Joe," Carrie said. "He's so incredible! You should have seen him dance!"

"Well, maybe we will," Amy said. "I'm having a party Saturday night, and you can bring him."

"What's the occasion?"

"No special occasion," Amy replied. "Just a get-together. And you'd better come—everyone's dying to hear about the video and Michael Jackson. Do you think Joe will want to come?"

"I'll ask," Carrie promised.

And she did—first thing Thursday morning. Joe looked pleased.

"Great," he said. "I'd like to meet your friends. And it'll be a nice change to be around people who *aren't* in the business!"

Carrie gave him a mischievous look. "Except—that's all they'll want to hear about!"

Joe gave a mock groan, and Carrie laughed sympathetically.

The studio was in total disarray that morning, with men building sets everywhere. Mac called them all together.

"You're getting a break today, kids," he announced. "You'll be fitted for your costumes this morning, and once you're done with that, you're off for the day. I want you to get a good rest because tomorrow's going to be a big day. We'll be having a full dress rehearsal, with costumes, sets, music, and"—he paused, then smiled—"Michael Jackson."

A squeal went up from some of the girls. Mac frowned slightly.

"Now I hope you'll all remember what I told you last week. Keep in mind that this is a professional music video you're making. So let's all act like professionals, OK? Now, girls, if you'll go upstairs, you'll find Ms. Lasky, who will be handling your wardrobe. Boys, go downstairs and . . ."

As Carrie followed the other girls, Joe ran after her. "I forgot to tell you," he said, "I can't take you home this afternoon. I've got an interview for that job at the hospital on the other side of town."

"That's OK," Carrie said. "I'll get a ride with Renee."

She looked for Renee in the wardrobe room and found her in an argument already with Ms. Lasky.

"But I don't *like* this dress," Renee was saying. "It's dull. I want something flashier."

Ms. Lasky's eyes narrowed, and she looked as if she was trying very hard to keep her temper under control.

"I'm sorry you don't like it," she said briskly. "But the costumes have already been selected and carefully coordinated."

"But—"

"No buts," Ms. Lasky said firmly, and she turned to Carrie. "And who are you?"

"Carrie Philips."

Ms. Lasky checked her list. "I'll get your outfits, and you can try them on. I *do* hope you'll like them," she added sarcastically, glancing at Renee.

"What's the matter with that dress?" Carrie asked, looking at Renee's outfit. It was a simple, flared green dress with a cute pointed collar.

"I wanted something sexier," Renee grumbled. "Michael will never notice me in this."

Carrie groaned. "Oh, Renee, you're not still thinking you're going to latch onto Michael Jackson."

"Why not?" she asked. "I've had pretty good luck with guys in the past."

Carrie stared at her. How could anyone be that smug? Was Renee for real?

"After all," Renee continued, "he may be a superstar, but he's still a guy, right?"

Carrie was at a loss for words. "Look," she said to change the subject, "can I get a ride home with you?" Renee agreed in her usual less-than-gracious way.

Ms. Lasky returned with Carrie's costumes. There was a cute red dress for the first three scenes and adorable purple overalls for the disco scene. Carrie tried them on, and Ms. Lasky made some adjustments in the hem of the overalls.

"They'll be ready for you in the morning,"

she said. "These are nice colors for you," she added.

Carrie got a glimpse of herself in the overalls in the mirror. She had to admit she looked pretty cute! She hoped Joe would agree.

Nina suddenly appeared beside her in the mirror. She was brushing her hair frantically and looking tense.

"What's up?" Carrie asked.

Nina smiled nervously. "I'm going to a big audition," she said. "It's a callback. I've already tried out once for the part. It's my first real chance at a big speaking part in a feature film, so I'm really excited." She grinned at Carrie. "It's for the part of a beauty contestant, so I've got to look good."

"You look great," Carrie said sincerely. "Good luck." She couldn't imagine anyone as pretty as Nina not getting a part as a beauty contestant.

Renee was waiting for her at the door of the wardrobe room. "Let's go," she said. "I want to get home. I've got a lot of reading to do."

Carrie wondered what kind of reading Renee had to do that was so important. She soon found out when she got into Renee's car. Piled in the back was a stack of magazines, and Carrie could see Michael Jackson on the cover of almost all of them.

"I've got to read every one of these," Renee said. "I want to know everything about him. Then I'll know what to talk to him about."

Carrie frowned. "Renee, you can't believe everything you read in those magazines."

Renee brushed that comment aside. "It's a way to begin a relationship," she said, her expression determined.

They didn't talk much on the way home. Several times Carrie tried to start conversations, but Renee was her usual unfriendly self. Carrie wondered about Renee—if she ever let anyone get close to her. At school Renee didn't seem to have any girlfriends—at least, Carrie never saw her with any. She was always with a guy, and she seemed to change boyfriends monthly. The girls, Carrie knew, either envied or disliked her. And Renee didn't seem particularly anxious to be anyone's friend—if anything, she treated all girls as enemies.

Carrie gave up on trying to make conversation, and they rode the rest of the way in silence.

The next day Carrie awoke feeling very excited. And when she got to the studio, she sensed she wasn't alone in this feeling—a spirit of overwhelming anticipation filled the air.

Carrie went to the wardrobe room first. As she slipped into the red dress, she saw Nina putting on her outfit.

"How was the audition?" Carrie asked.

"It went pretty well, I think," Nina replied. "I should find out in a few days if I got the part." She smiled at Carrie. "I'm trying not to think about it. I really want that part!"

"I'll bet you get it," Carrie said. The actress walked downstairs with her, and when they went into the main studio, Carrie gasped. It was transformed. Instead of a huge empty room, there were four large sets that looked amazingly authentic.

The classroom looked just like one in Carrie's high school. There were chairs with attached desks set up in rows, a big teacher's desk in the front, and a blackboard. The arcade set was lined with flashing video games. The restaurant looked like a typical hamburger joint, with big booths and signs that said things like "Super-Duper Burger $2.95." And the disco—well, Carrie had never seen one that looked so glamorous, but it was just the way she imagined a fancy disco would look. The walls were dark blue and sprinkled with glitter. It looked as if the room was surrounded by a midnight sky.

And there was Michael. He was dressed all in black—black pants and black crew neck sweater. His hands were in his pockets.

He didn't have his sunglasses on, and even from a distance, Carrie was mesmerized by those famous almond-shaped eyes. He was so incredibly handsome.

She was aware of Nina smiling at her in an understanding way. "He *is* gorgeous, isn't he?" she murmured. "Want to meet him?"

"I don't know," Carrie said hesitantly. "Mac said we shouldn't bother him—"

"That doesn't mean you can't say hello," Nina said. "Come on, I'll introduce you."

And Carrie, feeling as if she were walking in a dream, moved forward with Nina to meet Michael Jackson.

Chapter Nine

It only lasted a moment, but it was a moment Carrie knew she would remember forever. As she drew closer to him, she realized he was taller than she thought.

"Michael, this is Carrie Philips," Nina said and added, unnecessarily, "Carrie, this is Michael Jackson."

Carrie looked up into those famous eyes—deep, sensitive eyes that were warm, intelligent, and yet mysterious. He smiled, revealing brilliantly white, even teeth.

"Hello, Carrie," he said quietly, and he gently shook her hand. He seemed relaxed and sincere—not at all phony, the way Carrie had imagined famous people might be. It was a moment in which she felt suspended in time and space.

But the spell was broken in a flash when Renee appeared. Carrie's heart sank when she saw her standing there, poised like a cat ready to pounce. She had on what the girls at school called her "killer" smile, the one intended to drop guys dead in their tracks.

"Hi," she said to Michael. "Remember me?" The question was posed in such a way as to suggest no one could forget her.

But Michael just smiled. He nodded politely, murmured something and then turned to Mac, who had joined them.

"Let me show you the disco set," Mac said to him, and the two walked away.

Carrie looked at Nina, and then both of them turned toward Renee. The girl looked stricken, and Carrie almost felt sorry for her. Michael had spoken pleasantly to her, but Renee had obviously expected something more.

Renee's expression changed to one of careful nonchalance. "I'll catch up with him later," she said casually, tossing an I-don't-care look at Carrie and Nina. Carrie realized that Renee was embarrassed because she and

Nina had been witnesses to her unsuccessful flirtation.

Nina seemed to understand this, too. "Poor girl," she said. "Someone should tell her to give up trying to win Michael."

"Places, everyone!" Mac called out. Carrie and Nina walked quickly over to the classroom set.

As she took her seat and watched the other extras take their places, Carrie marveled at how different this rehearsal seemed. The realistic sets gave her a vivid sense of how the video would actually appear. And the costumes made everyone seem more alert, more excited. Also Michael's being there lifted everyone's energy level.

"OK, everyone," Mac said, "let's start with a complete run-through of the first sequence. This is your first time on the actual set, and it may feel awkward, but do your best."

The music began. And everyone was doing just what they had been directed to do. For Carrie, this meant simply staring, her elbow on the desk and her chin in her hand.

And then Michael appeared. Carrie tried to remember the "lovesick" look she had practiced, but she had a feeling her face was only reflecting what she felt—stunned.

His entrance was electric. He took a few light steps and whipped into a dazzling spin. Then he froze, and Renee and Lauren appeared on each side of him and took his arms. Quickly he glided forward, thrusting out his arms as if freeing himself from the girls. He whirled around, spotted Nina, and moved toward her with a rhythmic step. On cue Nina turned in her seat so her back was to Michael. The music stopped, and Mac came forward.

"Not bad,"-he said. "But there are a few problems we need to clear up. Lauren, you were a little slow again getting to Michael's side. Renee, just take his arm lightly, don't clutch. You were coming on too strong."

That's typical, Carrie thought. Her heart sank when she heard her own name next.

"Carrie, Mark, Brenda—your expressions were wrong. You were all gawking. Remember how you're supposed to be looking. Now, let's go through it again."

This time, even though Michael's dancing was just as fantastic, Carrie managed to act as she had been directed to do.

She was thrilled again when Michael danced in the video arcade sequence. There he entered with a swagger, snapping his fingers.

He wore a red-and-black T-shirt under a short, black leather jacket. His presence was so magnetic that Carrie knew it would be impossible to take her eyes off him—luckily, that's where they were supposed to be.

When they broke for lunch, she saw Renee run up to Michael immediately. She tried to talk to him—but within two seconds he was drawn away by studio people. Renee just stood there, looking frustrated.

Joe, Nina, and a couple of the other extras joined Carrie for lunch. No matter what direction the conversation took, it kept coming back to Michael's performance that morning.

"I've never seen anything like it," one girl said. "He's totally awesome." The boys in the group were equally impressed.

"Wow," one of them said, "what I wouldn't give to have that kind of talent."

"I wonder if there's anyone in the world who hasn't heard of him," Carrie mused.

"I doubt it," Lauren replied. "I can't imagine what it would be like to be so famous."

"Must be pretty wonderful," Mark Clinton said. "Wish *I* could find out what it's like."

"Maybe it's not so great," Joe said. "I think fame can really hurt a person's ability to come and go as he pleases. I mean, what kind of personal life can you have?"

Mark shrugged. "That's a small price to pay," he commented.

Joe frowned slightly. "I don't know," he said. "It couldn't be easy being a public person. Anything you did would be common knowledge. People would try to know everything about you."

He glanced at Carrie and smiled in an intimate way. "I like to think there are some things you share only with special people."

Carrie basked in the warmth of his smile. She knew what he meant, but she suspected he was exaggerating a bit about the price of fame. Surely stars had private lives. After all, she didn't know everything about Michael Jackson.

After lunch they rehearsed the restaurant scene. This time, Michael was wearing a light blue sweater over a white shirt. When he approached Renee at her booth, he did one of his famous spins, finishing with his foot on the edge of the table.

But it was the disco scene that really took everyone's breath away. Carrie and Joe had just done their little fancy step when, on the record, there was a crash of cymbals. At this point Michael leaped onto the dance floor. He was wearing a glittery red and gold jacket that reflected the lights. Every move he made was precise and sharp. He twirled three times and rose onto the points of his toes. Then he pointed to Nina, she moved toward him, and they began to dance together. The extras stepped backward silently. Mac had told them that at this point the cameras would focus solely on Michael and Nina. This time the extras could gape and gawk all they wanted.

And Michael's dancing was well worth the gaping. He was spectacular when he moved across the floor, as if he were floating on air. Carrie watched him with a feeling close to reverence.

When the record ended and the dancing stopped, there was a moment of silence. Then a spontaneous burst of applause erupted among the extras and the various members of the crew who had stopped their work to watch. Michael smiled and waved, graciously acknowledging the applause.

"What a thriller," Carrie murmured to Joe, and he agreed enthusiastically.

"He's got a real gift," he said.

Suddenly it seemed to be the right time to say what had been on her mind for the past week. "Joe," Carrie said, "you could be a thriller, too."

Joe pretended to look hurt. "Gee," he said, "I thought I already was."

Carrie rolled her eyes. "I mean, a thriller like Michael Jackson. You've got talent, too, you know."

Joe laughed. "Not like that," he said. "I couldn't be another Michael Jackson."

"Maybe not now," Carrie admitted. "But if you worked at it—"

Joe brushed her words aside and shook his head. "Come on, Carrie, that's not my style," he said. And before he could say more, Mac called them back to work.

It was a long day, an exhausting day, and Carrie went to bed early that evening. As she lay there, she drowsily thumbed through an old magazine. A picture caught her eye. It was a photo of Michael at the Grammy Awards with Brooke Shields. She stared at it for a minute, and in her mind, the faces in the photo changed. It was Joe behind the dark glasses, and she became the beautiful girl in the evening gown. With a sleepy giggle, Carrie tossed the magazine aside. But the picture reappeared in her dreams.

* * *

On Saturday evening Carrie dressed with special care for Amy's party. Her new jeans hugged her hips snugly, and her carefully ironed sleeveless yellow blouse fitted perfectly. A yellow- and blue-striped belt pulled the outfit together. The reflection in the mirror gave her real pleasure. Never before could she remember having felt this confident!

She couldn't wait to show Joe off to her friends. There was no doubt in her mind that her friends would like Joe, and vice versa—and she knew her friends would be happy to see her in such a happy relationship.

As that thought passed through her mind, she paused in the middle of brushing her hair. A relationship! That's what she and Joe were beginning to have. She'd never had one before, only dates, never any one boy in particular. But now she had Joe, and something very special was happening between them. She shivered with delight.

Joe picked her up promptly at eight, and this time she was ready. When she opened the door, he let out a soft whistle, and Carrie knew the mirror hadn't lied to her.

"You look fantastic," he said.

"So do you," Carrie replied. It was true—he did look fantastic. He had on a red-

and-white T-shirt with freshly pressed jeans; several curls fell casually down his forehead.

As they drove to Amy's, Carrie described some of the kids he'd be meeting. "They'll probably ask you a lot of questions about the famous people you've met," she said apologetically.

"I don't mind," Joe replied easily. "I'm used to that. Besides, I have to admit, I still get a kick out of meeting the big stars."

Amy greeted them at the door. Her eyes widened when she saw Joe.

"You must be Joe," she said. "Come on in!" As they walked in, Amy gave Carrie a wink that clearly said "I approve."

It was a terrific party. Carrie saw friends she hadn't seen since school let out, and they were all dying to hear about the video and Michael Jackson. Joe fit in perfectly.

"Carrie says you've been a back-up singer," Susan said. When Joe acknowledged this, the kids all began asking him questions. Joe entertained them with stories about this star and that star, and the group was enthralled.

Carrie loved the way Joe could tell his stories without sounding like a show-off. Her friends were not only impressed with him, they *liked* him, and Carrie felt very proud.

"Joe," she said impulsively, "how about singing something?" A couple of the kids echoed her suggestion.

Joe looked distinctly uncomfortable and begged off. "No, thanks," he said. "Personally, I'd rather listen to Michael Jackson. Or anyone, for that matter. Hey, Amy, do you have that album . . ." As he passed Carrie on the way to the stereo, he gave her a peculiar look. Carrie began to feel uneasy. Was something wrong?

Joe was unusually quiet on the way home.

"Joe," Carrie asked, "is everything OK?"

"Sure," he said, then paused. He looked as if he wanted to say something but was afraid. "Carrie," he began hesitantly, "I wish you hadn't asked me to sing tonight."

"Why not?" she asked, honestly puzzled.

"I was embarrassed," he said simply. "I just don't think of myself as a singer."

"But you've got talent—"

"That's not the point," he interrupted. "It's not the way I see myself, and it's not the way I want others to see me. Can you understand that?"

"I suppose so," Carrie said. "But when I

saw Michael performing yesterday, I kept thinking how wonderful it must feel to have such talent. You have talent, too, Joe, and—well, I guess I just wanted everyone to know." Even as the words left her lips, she was feeling ashamed of her own motives.

Joe was silent, and Carrie sighed. "Joe, I'm sorry," she said honestly. "I didn't mean to embarrass you. I guess I wasn't thinking."

"It's OK," he replied, smiling. "Carrie, I really like you. No, more than that." He gave a funny little cough. "Anyway," he continued, "I hope you, uh, feel the same."

"Oh, Joe, I do."

"The thing is, Carrie, I hope you care about me for who I am. Not because I sing a little or because of the recording work. Do you know what I mean?"

Carrie smiled. "I know exactly what you mean," she said. "It's not the singing and dancing I care about, Joe. What I like is—your warmth and your sense of humor and the way you really care about people. Also, you're real cute!"

Joe's face had relief written all over it. "I'm glad," he said quietly. "Because that's what I like about you, too." By now they were at Carrie's door.

"Or maybe," he said slowly, "that's what I love about you." Carrie closed her eyes. And this time their kiss lasted longer than ever before.

Chapter Ten

On Monday morning, the first day of actual taping, Carrie awoke feeling tense and unsure of herself. Just knowing a camera would be on her made her feel more than a little nervous.

"Carrie, we need to leave a little earlier this morning," her mother said at breakfast. "I've got a meeting at the office."

"That's fine, Mom," Carrie assured her. "I'll be so nervous it'll probably take me twice as long to get into my costume."

Even though she was almost an hour early arriving at the studio, the set was bustling with activity. Cameras were being moved about, and dozens of workers were adjusting props. Carrie was afraid she'd get in the way, so she went upstairs to the wardrobe room.

At first she thought the room was empty. Then she saw a still figure, sitting alone in a corner and staring out a window. It was Renee.

Carrie walked over to her. "What are you doing here so early?" she asked.

Renee turned toward her. She had a peculiar, almost vacant, expression on her face. "I thought I might run into Michael," she said in a dull voice. "I figured maybe I could talk to him."

"Did you see him?"

Renee nodded, then gave a short, bitter laugh. "He said hello and kept right on moving." She paused, and a look of despair came over her. "I can't understand it," she said in a bewildered voice. "I've never had a guy absolutely ignore me like that."

What an ego, Carrie thought. But at the same time she felt strangely sorry for the girl. "Gosh, Renee," she said. "Michael Jackson's not your ordinary guy. He's a big star."

"I know, I know," Renee said impatiently. "I figured he was sort of a challenge. I mean, if I could get Michael Jackson to notice me—"

Carrie interrupted. "Is it that important to you, Renee? I mean, getting guys to notice you?"

Renee shrugged. "Sure," she said. "What else is there?"

Carrie thought for a minute. "There's family," she said, "and friends—"

"You mean girlfriends?" Renee asked. "Who needs them? They're nothing but competition."

Carrie was shocked. "I can't believe you're saying that," she said, "Everyone needs friends to—to care about. Friends who will listen to your problems and share secrets and—"

"I wouldn't know," Renee said.

"Don't you have any friends?"

Renee shrugged again. "Girls don't like me," she said. "I threaten them." She sounded as if she was actually proud of that.

"You don't threaten me," Carrie said.

Renee smirked. "Oh, no? How would you feel if I started flirting with that Davenport guy you've been chasing?"

"I'm not chasing him," Carrie protested.

"Sure you are," Renee insisted. "You put me down for going after Michael, but you're doing the same thing with Joe."

"It's different with Joe and me."

"Oh, yeah? Why is it different?"

"Because we really care about each other," Carrie said simply.

Renee didn't say anything.

"Joe's special to me," Carrie continued. "He's not just some guy to go out with."

Renee stood up and began to move about restlessly. "All guys are alike," she said finally, dismissing the entire sex with a wave of her hand. "Some are better looking than others, that's all."

Carrie felt a combination of annoyance and amusement. "Oh, come on, Renee. I think you're just trying to shock me. You don't really believe that."

Renee whirled around. "How do *you* know what I believe?" she snapped. "You don't even know me."

"That's true," Carrie replied. "I don't."

The two girls stared at each other. Slowly Carrie began to realize something. It was all an act. Renee had cultivated an image of herself as the girl who could get any guy she wanted. And Renee was right—Carrie didn't know her. Carrie wondered if anyone knew what lay behind the mask Renee wore all the time.

"I don't know you," Carrie repeated. "I don't think anyone does."

Renee's eyes narrowed. "What are you getting at?"

"I think you're a fake," Carrie said boldly. "You put on this sexy, I-can-get-any-guy routine, and it's all an act. I think you're hiding something."

"Oh, yeah? What?"

"I don't know," Carrie replied honestly.

Again the girls just looked at each other. By then, other cast members were coming into the room, and the wardrobe mistress was calling out names to go next door for makeup.

"Carrie Philips?"

"Coming," Carrie called out, then turned to Renee.

"If you ever get sick of your act," she said impulsively, "come and talk to me, OK? You just might need a friend after all."

Then she left—but not before she noticed a slight change in Renee's expression. For a second the arrogant girl had looked almost wistful.

Seated in the makeup room, Carrie was oblivious to the excited chatter around her and to the hands that were swiftly applying creams and powders to her face. She was thinking about Renee, but this time, with pity. So many times Carrie had wanted to be different, to stand out, to be someone else. They were just fantasies, though, daydreams—deep in her heart she really didn't mind just being Carrie Philips. But Renee acted out her fantasies—and Carrie didn't think she was really very happy about it.

"There!" said the makeup man. "Take a look at yourself."

Carrie did and gasped. Talk about fantasies! The girl who returned her stare in the mirror was—stunning! Her complexion was flawless, her eyes looked huge, her lips had an iridescent glow. She even had cheekbones!

"Is that really me?" she cried.

The makeup man laughed. "The miracle of modern cosmetic science! Yes, that's really you—with a little enhancement."

As she went back into the wardrobe room, Carrie passed Renee, who walked by as if she didn't even see Carrie. And again Carrie wondered what kind of person Renee really was.

On the set cameras were still being pushed about as the camera people tested different angles. Over a loudspeaker a voice called, "Everyone on the set for scene one." There was a man walking around with a walkie-talkie in his hand, and he was muttering into it. Jeff Drummond, the assistant director, was wearing a headset. Carrie asked him what the headset was for.

"That's how I hear Mac's instructions," Mr. Drummond replied.

Carrie looked around. "Where *is* Mac?"

The assistant director pointed to a window high up on a wall facing the set. "He's up there, watching everything on a monitor. That's how he can tell how a scene will look on the screen. You guys will be able to hear him on the loudspeaker."

The man with the walkie-talkie walked by.

"Who's he?" Carrie asked.

"He's in charge of lights," Mr. Drummond replied. "He uses that to talk to the lighting people."

Carrie had no idea so many people would be on the set for filming—and watching, she thought with a sinking feeling.

But just then she saw Joe, and her heart lifted.

"Hey, you look terrific," he said to her.

Carrie spun around in her bright red dress and struck a pose. "Think I could break into the big time?"

Joe grinned. "You already have. You're my girl, aren't you?"

Carrie groaned and Joe laughed. "Nervous?" he asked.

"A little," Carrie admitted. "How about you?"

"A little," Joe agreed. "But I'm feeling great! I had some good news yesterday."

"What happened?"

But before he could reply, a voice came over the loudspeaker. "Extras in position for scene one, take one."

"I'll tell you later," Joe promised, and they separated to join the others on the set.

As Carrie slid into her seat, she looked at Nina, who was already in her position in the next seat.

"Hi!" Carrie said.

The actress returned the greeting, but her normally vivacious face looked unusually solemn.

"Is something wrong?" Carrie asked uncertainly.

Nina smiled weakly. "Remember the audition I told you about?"

"Sure! What happened?"

"Well, I didn't get the part."

Carrie's mouth fell open. "You're kidding! Why not?"

Nina shrugged. "Who knows? There was probably someone a little prettier, a little more talented, whatever." She gave a dry laugh. "That's show biz."

"I'm sorry," Carrie said sympathetically.

Nina made a face. "Thanks. You'd think by now I'd be used to disappointments. After all, this is probably the zillionth job I didn't get." She paused. "But you never get used to it."

Carrie didn't know what to say. She couldn't understand how someone like Nina couldn't get any part she wanted. Carrie began to wonder suddenly what Joe's "good news" was—maybe Mac had signed him up to do another video with some other rock star! But her thoughts were interrupted by the whisper of an extra behind her.

"There he is."

Carrie turned her head and saw Michael standing next to Jeff Drummond, just off the set. He was wearing the black pants and sweater she had seen him in at the rehearsal. They made his lithe body seem even more slender. And even though she'd seen him several times, each time was a new thrill. Even in repose, his body seemed charged with energy.

As he talked with Mr. Drummond, he smiled, and it was like a burst of sunlight. The huge lights on the set were bright, but

Michael's smile was brighter. The girl behind Carrie sighed, and Carrie mentally echoed it.

"Are we all ready?" the assistant director asked loudly. A murmur of assent went up from the set, and then the voice came over the speakers.

"Scene one, take one. Action!"

Carrie automatically fell into her bored-in-class expression, her elbow on the desk and her chin in her hand. Her heart was pounding so loudly she thought everyone must be able to hear it. Then the music started.

Michael entered with his light, rhythmic step. Carrie turned and concentrated on looking lovesick. Michael looked so incredibly wonderful that her expression felt perfectly natural.

He whipped into a spin and then froze. Renee and Lauren took his arms, and he thrust them away in one graceful movement. It was all perfectly timed—but Renee stumbled.

"Cut!" Renee looked completely confused. Jeff Drummond was speaking to her quietly.

Then the voice came on again. "Scene one, take two. Action!"

This time Lauren made a mistake—she took Michael's arm a second before Renee did.

"Cut!"

And so it went, take after take. In one take, someone moved when he shouldn't; in another, Nina didn't turn her back quickly enough. Only Michael never did anything wrong. In each take his performance was exquisite.

There was a break after five takes. All the extras looked exhausted. Carrie joined Joe for a sandwich and soda.

"How can it take all day to film one minute?" she asked.

"Mac's a perfectionist," Joe said. "And so is Michael. We'll be doing this till it's absolutely perfect." He groaned. "I'm beat."

"Everyone is," Carrie said. "Except Michael. He's amazing. How does he do it?"

"He's a professional," Joe replied simply.

"I've never seen anyone like him," Carrie said. "He's like—magic."

"Mmm," Joe murmured. "Hey, I didn't tell you my news! I got the part-time job at the hospital!"

Carrie knew she should feel excited for him. And she *was* honestly pleased. Still, working in a hospital certainly didn't sound as interesting as working in the music business. She did manage to smile warmly and say

131

"That's great, Joe." But she couldn't help asking, "Do you think you'll still have time to do any recording work?"

Joe brushed that aside. "Probably—though not so much. Anyway, I'm just so excited about this job, I can't think of anything else right now."

The voice over the speaker called them back onto the set.

On the next take, Carrie thought the scene was perfect, and no one yelled cut in the middle of it. But there were two more takes. Carrie was beginning to feel as if the lovesick expression was permanently fixed on her face, and if she never heard that first minute of the record again, it would be too soon.

But each of Michael's performances was as good, if not better than the last. Each move was dazzling, brilliant—like a flash of lightning. Each step was precise, razor sharp. And in his expressions, there was—everything. Intelligence, humor, warmth—

"Cut!"

And that was it—finally. Carrie felt stiff as she rose from her chair.

She began to walk off the set and noticed that Renee was still standing in her position. Her face was expressionless.

"Renee?"

The girl's eyes focused, and she looked at Carrie. "Yeah?"

Carrie hesitated. She wasn't even sure what she wanted to say to her. "I thought you did really well today," she said.

Renee looked puzzled, as if she'd never heard a compliment before. She was silent.

"Well, I'll see you later," Carrie finally said and turned away.

"Wait!"

Carrie turned around. Renee had an odd half smile on her face. It looked almost sincere.

"Thanks." And then, as if she had said something terrible, she turned and walked rapidly in the opposite direction.

Carrie went back to the wardrobe room to change and take off her makeup. When she came out, Joe was waiting for her.

As they left the studio, Carrie was feeling a little out of it. She was exhausted—who would have thought that sitting still and looking lovesick could make a person feel so tired?—yet she felt strangely exhilarated. She couldn't stop thinking about Michael's brilliant performances.

"If I had to describe him," she told Joe, "I couldn't. He's beyond words."

"Right," Joe said, but his thoughts were obviously elsewhere. "Hey, you know what they told me at the hospital? They said I might get a chance to observe some operations, if the doctors say it's OK."

"That's nice," Carrie said without much enthusiasm.

"You don't sound very interested," Joe said, sounding almost hurt.

"Oh, I am," Carrie said quickly. "I guess I'm just still thinking about the taping. You were so good, Joe! Maybe Michael Jackson will want you to be in his next one."

"Maybe," Joe said. "I sure could use the money. If I'm going to get into one of the really good medical schools, I need to go to a first-rate college."

"Maybe," Carrie said carefully, "once you start working in the hospital, you might find out that being a doctor isn't what you want after all."

"I doubt that," Joe said and paused to look at Carrie curiously. "How come all of a sudden you're so down on my being a doctor?"

"I'm not down on it," Carrie objected hastily. She remembered something a guidance counselor at school had told her. "I just think you ought to keep your options open."

Joe was quiet. "Look, Carrie," he said finally, "if you mean I should think about a singing career—I don't know. I just don't feel like that's right for me. Even if I had the talent, I don't really want that kind of life-style. And the kind of struggling someone like Nina has to go through—I wouldn't want that. I'd rather have a clear-cut goal that I know I can achieve. Do you know what I mean?"

"Sure," she said and hoped she sounded convincing. "Now, tell me more about what you'll actually be doing at the hospital."

Joe launched into a description of his duties, but Carrie only half listened. Once again she began to daydream about the day on the set. The image of a dazzling superstar swept across her mind. But was it Michael she was seeing? Funny—the vision kept turning into Joe.

Chapter Eleven

By the time she got to the studio on Tuesday, Carrie was beginning to feel as if she'd been taping for years. And she was also beginning to realize how much she'd miss the whole experience.

She thought back to her conversation with Amy the night before.

"I don't want it to end," Carrie had told her friend. "I mean, it's a lot of hard work and all that, but still, there's something about being around the studio and Michael Jackson and the other performers. The costumes, the makeup, the lights—there's always excitement. I wish it could all just go on and on."

"Maybe it can," Amy said. "Maybe you

should start thinking about that sort of career."

"In music videos?" Carrie laughed. "I don't think there are many jobs for professional extras. I can't sing or dance—and if someone as talented and beautiful as Nina can't get work, I sincerely doubt that I'd be bombarded with offers! Besides," she continued, "it's not actually being onstage that I care about. It's the atmosphere—"

"Maybe Joe will get another video job," Amy suggested. "Then at least you'd have a chance to be near all the excitement."

"That's what I'm hoping," Carrie confessed. "Joe's so talented. Honestly, Amy, I think he could be another Michael Jackson."

"Oh, come on, Carrie," Amy protested. "There's no such thing as another Michael Jackson."

"But I do think Joe could be a big star if he tried."

"But he's not interested in that kind of career."

"That's what he *says*. I wish I could convince him that he's got too much talent to waste."

"But he really wants to be a doctor," Amy reminded her.

"I know," Carrie said. "And being a doctor is a wonderful thing. But to be a star! That's something else. I keep thinking maybe he's just afraid of going for it, you know?"

"Maybe," Amy said, but there was doubt in her voice. "Or maybe he honestly doesn't *want* to be a star."

That suspicion rested uneasily in the back of Carrie's mind. After all, that was what Joe kept telling her—but she just wasn't convinced that he really meant it.

"I can't believe anyone wouldn't want to be a star if he could," she stated firmly.

"Well," Amy said finally, "you know him better than I do."

That's right, Carrie told herself. She knew Joe. And she could help him to realize what he really wanted. What he *should* want.

Or what you want him to want, said a small voice from the back of her mind. Carrie quickly pushed that notion aside.

But how was she going to convince him? That was the central question on her mind as she went through makeup and wardrobe on Tuesday morning. She'd have to be subtle about it. If she was too pushy, he'd be completely turned off. Maybe she could just casually point out the positive aspects of a performing career. And there were lots of positive features she could emphasize if she could think of ways to work them into a conversation. Maybe during their lunch break . . .

"All extras on the set! Now, please!"

Carrie walked down to the set with Nina, who was looking much more cheerful. "I've got another audition this afternoon," she told Carrie.

"Great!" Carrie said. "I hope you get this one."

Nina shrugged. "Who knows?" she said. "If I don't, I'll just be depressed for a day. And then I'll have another audition to worry about."

Carrie shivered. It all sounded a little gruesome to her. She couldn't imagine having to go through life getting knocked down on a daily basis. Nina must be pretty tough, she decided. If Carrie were in her place, the first time she got knocked down, she'd probably remain right where she landed permanently.

The video arcade set looked terrific. Carrie realized that all the game machines were real. They'd been hooked up. With their flashing colored lights and little objects running across the screens, the games made the set come alive even before it was peopled.

Michael was already there, sitting quietly, alone for once, almost hidden behind a camera. For a moment she felt an urge to walk over and talk to him. She wanted to ask him if he was happy with his life—if he ever regretted becoming a star. She wanted to be able to say to Joe, "Look, a superstar has a wonderful life."

But something told her not to bother him. He seemed to have so few moments alone.

Suddenly she wondered where Renee was. Surely if she had seen Michael sitting alone, she would have headed straight for him.

Carrie looked around the set, and to her surprise, she saw that Renee was already in her place. She was standing alone beside a video game, staring at nothing, and she wasn't even looking at Michael. Carrie thought about going over to speak to her, but at that moment she saw Joe coming toward her.

She waved to him, but just as he was halfway across the set, the announcement came over the loudspeaker that they were ready to begin shooting. Joe shrugged good-naturedly and mouthed "later."

Carrie's eyes followed him. He was really

so good-looking. Even in his plain jeans and blue shirt, he stood out among the other guys.

"He's awfully cute," whispered Lauren, who had taken her place next to Carrie. Carrie smiled and nodded in agreement.

"He can really move, too," Lauren continued. "I saw him practicing the disco scene. I think he's got talent."

Carrie felt pleased that someone else had noticed how special Joe was. It wasn't just her imagination—Joe *did* have star quality!

During the next hour, Carrie thought if she heard the word "cut" one more time she'd scream. She couldn't believe how many things could go wrong in a simple scene. First, an extra moved in the wrong direction and bumped into someone. Then, one of the video games conked out, and the screen went blank. Mac really was a perfectionist—one cut was because someone's shoelace had come untied.

When Michael came onto the set, swaggering and snapping his fingers, one girl was supposed to faint and be caught by a guy. They had done it perfectly in rehearsal—but this time the boy missed, letting the poor girl land on the floor. Luckily she wasn't hurt, but the makeup man had to dash on the set and redo her.

Throughout all this, Michael was patient and never showed any sign of irritation. Each time he performed the short dance routine enchantingly. What a glorious effect Michael had on people! It dawned on Carrie that *this* was the facet of performing she should stress with Joe—the happiness that a great performer gives people.

She appreciated Joe's desire to do something for others; but what could be more satisfying than bringing them happiness?

Finally they made it through a whole take without any mistakes.

"You've got forty-five minutes for lunch," Jeff Drummond announced. "Then, back on the set for another take."

Carrie got her sandwich and soda and looked around for Joe. At first she didn't see him.

"Have you seen Joe?" she asked Mark Clinton, who had joined her.

"He's over there, talking to some man."

Carrie looked in the direction Mark indicated and saw Joe deep in conversation with a man she didn't recognize.

"Who is he?" she asked Mark.

"Don't know," Mark said. "But I think,

maybe, he's somebody important. I saw him talking with Michael Jackson a while back."

The strange man did look important. Carrie wasn't quite sure why—but he had an executive look.

Their conversation didn't last very long. Carrie had only taken a couple of bites of her sandwich when she saw Joe walking toward them. He was looking amused and shaking his head ruefully. When he reached them, he said, "Boy, some people won't take no for an answer."

"Who was that?" Mark asked.

Joe grimaced. "His name's Gramden, or Cramston, something like that. He's some big shot from a record company."

"Oh, yeah?" Mark said eagerly. "I think I'll go introduce myself." He sauntered off in that direction, and Carrie turned to Joe.

"What was he talking to you about?"

Joe looked half flattered, half embarrassed. "Mac told him I did some of the back-up singing on this record. He asked me if I was interested in cutting a demo."

"A what?"

"Oh, it's a record you cut," Joe explained. "And then record company people listen to it and decide if they want to give you a contract."

Carrie's eyes widened. "Joe, how exciting! Congratulations!"

Joe's eyes narrowed, and he looked at Carrie seriously. "Carrie, I told him no."

"What!"

Joe seemed puzzled by the surprise in Carrie's voice. "Cutting a demo is a lot of work. It's only for serious singers."

"But—but Joe! How can you pass up an opportunity like this? This could be your big break!"

Joe stared at her. "Carrie, I'm not looking for a big break. I've told you before, I'm not interested in a singing career."

It was what she had dreamed of for Joe! Visions of Joe onstage, of his picture on an album and the cover of *Rolling Stone*, and of his accepting a Grammy, with her on his arm. They were all fantasies, but there was a chance they could all come true. And Joe had just destroyed all those dreams!

"Joe, how could you do that!" she burst out. "It's the chance of a lifetime! You can't turn it down! Joe, you could be a star!"

"I don't want to be a star," he said quietly. "Haven't you heard me?"

"I've heard you," Carrie replied heatedly. "But I think you're just afraid of trying. You've got talent, Joe. You say you want to do something for people—it's your obligation to share your talent!"

"I'll be a better doctor than a singer," Joe said in a flat, even voice.

"But, Joe—" Carrie began and then stopped. There was a look in his eyes that frightened her. What was it?

In the silence that followed, she frantically tried to think of some way to change his mind. She took a deep breath. Fighting to keep her voice under control, she said, "I only want success for you."

"That's not true," he replied coldly. "You want it for yourself." With that, he turned abruptly and walked away.

Carrie stood frozen, unable to move. That look in his eyes—she knew what it was. It was disappointment and hurt. As if in slow motion, she walked to a trash can and threw her half-eaten sandwich away. She wasn't hungry anymore.

Chapter Twelve

Carrie drifted through the last taping of the day as if in a fog, barely aware of what she was doing. She couldn't bring herself to even glance at Joe—and when the scene was finished, she ran straight back to the wardrobe room. All she wanted to do was change her clothes and get home as fast as she could, without having to talk to anyone.

As she was tying her shoelaces, a voice asked, "Need a ride home?"

Carrie looked up and saw Renee standing there. "OK. Thanks."

This was the first time Renee had ever offered her a ride. But Carrie was too hazy to contemplate why the girl had stepped out of character. Silently she followed Renee out of the studio and into the parking lot.

When they got into the car, Renee glanced at Carrie curiously. "You OK?"

"Yes," Carrie lied.

As they drove off, Carrie stared straight ahead, but she was aware that Renee kept glancing at her.

"Is something wrong between you and Joe?" she asked finally. "I mean, you usually leave with him."

Carrie didn't feel like answering, but she knew she had to say something. "We—we had a little argument," she managed to say. "To be honest, I really don't much feel like talking about it. OK?"

"OK." And they rode the rest of the way in silence.

Again, Carrie vaguely sensed that something was different about Renee. But she couldn't think about that now. All she could think about was getting home, being alone, and trying to sort out the mess she had just made.

The house was silent; Carrie went straight to her room, feeling numb. She sank down on her bed and stared at her wall. It was a few minutes before she realized she was staring at her Michael Jackson poster. Suddenly she hated it. It was a reminder of everything she had just lost.

She leaped from her bed, tore the poster from the wall, and crumpled it up furiously.

And then the tears came. With the crumpling of the poster, the wall she had built around her emotions crumpled, too. She sank back onto her bed and wept. What had she done? How had she managed, in one brief conversation, to destroy the greatest happiness of her life? If only she had been more subtle, less insistent.

Finally there were no more tears, and she lay on her bed very still. The numbness had worn off, and now she was feeling the real pain.

The ring of the doorbell made her jump. Carrie lifted herself from the bed and looked out her front bedroom window. Susan and Amy were standing on her doorstep.

Go away, Carrie pleaded silently. She didn't want to talk to anybody—not even her best friends. But then Susan looked up, saw Carrie's face in the window, and waved. Now Carrie had to answer the door.

"It's about time," Amy said and then stopped. "Carrie! What's wrong?"

She hadn't thought she had any tears left, but she was wrong. As she poured out the dreary story to her friends, her eyes filled.

"I don't think he'll ever want to see me again," she told them. "I couldn't believe how angry he was. And I don't even know what I did that was so terrible."

Susan offered a possible explanation. "Maybe he thinks you were only going out with him because he might become a big star."

"But that's not true," Carrie protested. "I'd care about Joe no matter what he does. I just hate to see him waste his talent."

"Just because a person's got talent doesn't mean he has to use it," Amy said mildly. "I mean, there's no law that says just because you can sing, you have to be a singer."

"I know that," Carrie snapped. Then she sighed. "I'm sorry, Amy. I guess I'm just too upset to think."

"You've got to let him know you really like him for himself," Susan said. "Not just because he can sing and dance."

"I know, but how? He probably won't even listen. Besides," she added obstinately, "I still think he's making a mistake."

Amy and Susan were silent. The glance they exchanged told Carrie they didn't agree with her, but she was in no mood to argue with them.

For the first time ever, she was glad to see her friends leave. Why didn't they understand? Why couldn't they see she only wanted what was best for Joe?

Her thoughts were interrupted by the phone. Her heart leaped. Maybe it was Joe calling to say he'd thought it over and she was right.

"Hello?"

"Hi, honey, it's me."

"Oh. Hi, Mom."

"Carrie, are you all right? Your voice sounds funny."

Carrie resisted an impulse to tell her story again. She was afraid she'd just start crying and upset her mother.

"It's nothing, Mom. I'm just tired."

"Well, I'm calling to tell you I'll be home late. Some clients are here from out of town, and I need to take them out to dinner."

"OK." Secretly, Carrie was glad. She'd have time to calm down before her mother was home.

"There's sandwich stuff in the refrigerator," her mother was saying.

"OK," Carrie repeated. There was a pause.

"Carrie, are you sure nothing's wrong?" Her voice was concerned.

Carrie bit her lip. She felt as if she wanted to scream, but she somehow managed to reply calmly, "Nothing's wrong, Mom. But I might be in bed by the time you get home. I'm really beat."

"Well, OK. I'll see you in the morning then," her mother said.

The morning. Carrie contemplated having to go back to the studio and see Joe. How would she get through it?

She woke the next morning with a headache and still feeling depressed. The only good thing about the headache was that it provided her with an excuse for not being too lively at breakfast or in the car on the way to the studio.

As Mrs. Philips pulled into the studio parking lot, she said, "Carrie, I know something's bothering you, and it's not just a headache. Maybe you don't feel like talking about it now. But I want you to know that when you do feel like talking about it, I'll be glad to listen."

It was all Carrie could do to keep from bursting into tears again. "Thanks, Mom," she said unevenly. "I'll remember that."

It was early, and she hoped that she'd be alone in the wardrobe room so she could get her makeup and costume on without having to chat with the other girls.

But no such luck. Renee was already there. Carrie forced a halfhearted smile. "Looking for Michael again?"

To her astonishment, Renee actually smiled, and it looked sincere. "No," she said, "not this time. Actually, I was hoping to find you."

"Me?"

Renee nodded. "I've been thinking about what you said the other day. About how I was putting on an act, not being myself. . . ." She paused, looked down, and self-consciously twisted a lock of hair. Whatever she was trying to say, Carrie could tell it wasn't easy for her.

"I didn't mean to hurt your feelings," Carrie said, but Renee shook her head.

"No, not at all," she said. "No one has ever talked to me like that before. I don't have any girlfriends and—well—if it wasn't for all my dates, I'd be pretty lonely."

Carrie began to feel sorry for her. "It

doesn't have to be like that, Renee," she said gently. "You could have friends, you know?"

"Then why don't I?" Renee asked suddenly.

Carrie thought for a minute. Should she be honest? Might as well, she decided—the girl needed help. "Maybe because you come on so strong with the guys," she said slowly. "And that's sort of threatening, you know? You said that yourself, remember? And you don't seem to care who you hurt in the process."

"I know," Renee said softly. "When I was a kid, I was fat, and all the girls used to make fun of me. I lost a lot of weight a couple of years ago, and when all the guys at school started asking me out, I began to feel, well, sort of special and important. Being popular with the boys was everything to me. I mean, I really worked at it."

Carrie thought about this. "Maybe if you didn't work at it," she said, "maybe if you could just relax and be yourself—I know you could have friends."

"You think so?" Renee asked. "You don't think I've completely blown it with my reputation?"

Carrie shook her head firmly. "Reputations can be changed," she said. "You just have to put some effort into it. I'll help you."

"Really?" A little smile appeared.

Carrie was amazed. Who would have thought the famous Renee could feel insecure about herself?

"Sure," she said. "You've just got to let people know you. Then they'll appreciate you for you. But first, you have to respect and like yourself. You have to think about who you really are and stop thinking about what kind of impression you're making."

Renee nodded. She had a faraway look in her eyes. "When a guy pays attention to me," she said wistfully, "I always feel important. So when Michael ignored me, I felt like a failure."

"That's nonsense," Carrie said briskly. "I mean, we're not talking about any guy here. He's not just a star, he's a superstar, and when you're that hot, you have to protect yourself."

"I suppose so," Renee said and then laughed. "I guess this time I set goals that were just too high—even for me!" And she made a mock flirtatious face, batted her eyelashes, and stroked her blond hair seductively. Carrie began to laugh and knew she was making a new friend.

"*Be yourself*," she had told Renee, and then, suddenly, with a shock of recognition, she knew what she had done to Joe. She hadn't let him be himself; she had tried to force him to be someone else, an imitation of Michael Jackson.

The realization made her feel sick.

Joe was right—she had wanted it for herself. Selfishly, she had wanted Joe to be a star, not because it would make him happy, but because she, Carrie, wanted to be close to the glitter and glamour of a celebrity world. She had wanted to live in reflected glory.

Somehow she managed to get through the day. Every now and then, she snuck glances at Joe. Once she felt him looking at her, but as soon as she met his eyes, he turned away.

The taping went smoothly, and for the first time they were finished by lunch. In the flurry of activity that followed the announcement of the final cut, Carrie looked for Joe. She didn't know what she'd say. She didn't even know if he would listen—but she had to try.

"Mark, have you seen Joe?"

"I think he's already gone," Mark said.

"What's the matter with him, anyway? I couldn't get a word out of him today."

Carrie didn't bother to answer. Still in her makeup and costume, she dashed off the set, down the hall, and out to the parking lot.

But she was too late. She was just in time to see Joe's car pulling out of the lot.

Depressed, she walked slowly back into the studio and up to the makeup room to wash her face. Nina was there, brushing her hair. Carrie felt the need to talk to someone a little older.

"Nina," she said hesitantly, "do you have a minute?"

The actress turned to her and smiled. "Sure," she said, "what's up? I noticed you were looking a little down today."

Carrie took a deep breath and told Nina the whole story.

"I was wrong," she said. "I know that now."

Nina's expression was sympathetic. "You're right," she said. "I mean, you're right in thinking that you're wrong." She perched on the edge of a sink and looked at Carrie intently. "Not everyone's cut out for this kind of life," she said gently. "Joe's got his own

157

dreams, his own plans. And if you really care about him, you'll respect that."

"I know," Carrie said softly. And now, what? If she told Joe she understood, if she apologized, would he care? Would it make any difference? She tried to feel hopeful, but it wasn't easy. She had a wretched feeling Joe would only listen politely, and then it would be over forever.

Nina hopped off the sink, gave Carrie a quick hug, and said, "Don't worry. Just talk to Joe, tell him you understand. Everything will be all right."

Carrie forced a small smile and thanked her. But as she mechanically began to remove her makeup, she suspected that Nina's prediction was a little too optimistic.

She examined her own reflection in the mirror. "Carrie Philips," she murmured aloud, "you blew it."

Chapter Thirteen

"I can't believe this is the last day," Carrie said as she pushed her breakfast around on her plate. Mrs. Phillips smiled sympathetically.

"I know you're going to miss all the excitement," she said. "It's been quite an experience, hasn't it?"

Carrie grimaced. "In more ways than one." She and her mother exchanged an understanding look. The night before, Carrie had told her mother about the argument with Joe. She did feel calmer now—still sad, but able to face the day.

"I'm sorry about you and Joe," Mrs. Phillips said gently. "But you never know—maybe you'll be able to work it out."

Carrie shook her head. "I don't think so,

Mom. I've been really stupid, and I'm just going to have to live with it." She managed a small smile. "At least I've learned my lesson. That's the last time I'll try to change someone to fit my fantasies!"

On the way to the studio, they talked about other things—mostly, what Carrie would do for the rest of the summer. Amy's family had invited her to join them for a week at the beach, which would be fun. Also, she'd go back to dance class—that would be nice, too. She'd get together with friends, read some books. All in all, it could turn out to be a pretty good summer.

But there'd be no more video, no more cameras, costumes, and makeup. No Michael Jackson. And worst of all, no more Joe.

She and Joe had talked about the summer, and they'd made plans. Bike rides, the beach, Disneyland—a pang went through her as she thought of what might have been.

"Carrie? We're here."

Carrie pushed her thoughts aside and said goodbye to her mother. As she opened the door to get out, her mother reached over and patted her hand.

"Carrie," she said, smiling, "I know this is hard to believe, but it's not the end of the world. And remember—any experience that you learn something from is a valuable one."

Carrie returned the smile. "I know, Mom," she said warmly. "And thanks."

Several extras were already there, running in and out of the makeup and wardrobe rooms. There was the usual flurry of activity, but somehow it all seemed more subdued. Carrie figured everyone was feeling a little sad as they contemplated the last day of shooting.

As she pulled on the purple overalls, she spotted Renee coming back from makeup and waved to her.

Renee echoed Carrie's words at breakfast: "I can't believe this is the last day."

Carrie grinned at her. "It's really been amazing, hasn't it?" Carrie said. "Just think, we've actually worked with Michael Jackson. And every time we see him on TV or hear him on the radio, we'll remember this."

And I'll think of Joe, she added to herself silently. She wondered if she'd ever be able to hear a Michael Jackson song without thinking of Joe.

"Extras on the set! Now, please!"

Carrie could feel her heart pounding rapidly as she ran down the steps to the set. They would be filming the disco scene, and she'd be face to face with Joe. Was there anything she could say to him? And even if she could think of something to say—would he listen?

Joe was already on the set, in position for the scene. He looked so handsome in his black jeans and black jacket. The lighting cast a glow on him that made his curly hair shine.

"Places, everyone," Mr. Drummond called out.

Carrie felt sure Joe would be able to see that she was shaking all over. Or maybe she was only shaking inside.

"Hello, Joe."

His expression wasn't unfriendly, but it wasn't very warm, either.

"Hello, Carrie."

She didn't have time to worry about what she'd say next. Mac had come down on the set to call for everyone's attention.

"OK, kids, this is the most difficult scene we'll be doing, so we'll probably have to do a number of takes. Let's run through the opening part before Michael enters."

The music started, and they began dancing. Carrie felt awkward and uncoordinated, and she couldn't bring herself to look at Joe. When they had to do their special dance bit, she stumbled. Flushed with embarrassment, she managed a quick glance at Joe. He didn't look very comfortable, either.

Mac made them run through the opening part several more times. Carrie forced herself to concentrate, not to think about her dancing partner. But it wasn't easy.

Mac was beginning to get impatient. "This isn't looking good," he said irritably. "There's no spirit! Let's run through it again. And this time I want to see some sparkle!"

All right, Carrie thought grimly. *I may not be a professional actress, but for the next thirty seconds I'm going to fake it.* She smiled brilliantly at Joe. He looked startled.

They started to dance. In the lyrics of the song, the boy beseeched the girl of his dreams: "Don't listen to what they say, I'm not that way at all, Love me for myself. . . ."

Carrie had heard the song over and over again, but this time that one line—"Love me for myself"—had real significance. Her phony smile faded, and she gazed directly into Joe's eyes. Did he hear it, too? Could he see what she hoped her eyes were saying?

Mac was pleased with that take and said they'd do one more with Michael's entrance. Michael leaped onto the dance floor, resplendent in his red and gold jacket. As Nina moved toward him, the extras began to slowly move backward.

Once off the set they whispered among themselves as they watched Michael and Nina. Someone behind Carrie said, "He really is a thriller."

Carrie turned slightly and smiled at Renee. "He is," Carrie replied quietly. "And he's one of a kind." But as the words left her lips, she knew she wasn't just thinking of Michael.

And then it was over. Mac's booming voice echoed across the set. "Cut! That's a wrap!"

A spontaneous cheer erupted. Suddenly people were hugging and kissing, laughing and crying.

Renee stood alone, and Carrie could see tears in her eyes. Impulsively, she threw her arms around the girl and gave her a quick hug.

"I don't want it to end," Renee was saying.

"There'll be more good times," Carrie promised. "There's still a whole summer ahead of us. I want you to meet my friends, and you can hang out with us."

There was a hint of a smile on Renee's face. "Do you think they'll like me?" she asked uncertainly.

"Sure they will," Carrie replied confidently. "Just be yourself."

Then she was swept up in more hugs—from Lauren, Mark, Nina . . .

"OK, everyone! Let's party!" With Mac's words, tables were rolled onto the set, and food appeared. There was music playing, and soon everyone was eating or dancing. Mark Clinton grabbed Carrie's hand, and they started dancing. The atmosphere was festive, and despite her heartache, Carrie felt herself caught up in the celebration.

Suddenly there was a commotion just off the set, near the exit. Several people had gathered, and Carrie could hear shouting.

"What's going on?" she asked Mark.

"I don't know," he replied. "Let's go see."

They joined the group by the door, and Carrie immediately saw what had happened. Some kids, obviously Michael Jackson fans, had managed to sneak into the studio. One of them was trying to grab Michael's hair as a bodyguard pulled her back. Another guard was pulling off another fan who had a firm hold on Michael's jacket.

There were probably only four or five of them, but they seemed like a mob. Carrie was horrified. They were acting like crazy people.

The uproar lasted only a few seconds before the fans were ejected from the studio. But Carrie stood there longer, stunned by what she had witnessed. If the guards hadn't responded so quickly, there was no telling what the so-called fans would have done to Michael.

"That's awful," she said aloud to herself.

"Yes, it is," said a familiar voice behind her. Carrie turned and faced Joe.

He was looking at her intently, and his eyes were troubled. "I could never live like that," he said simply.

Suddenly Carrie knew exactly what she had to say. "I know," she said softly. "And I'm sorry, Joe. I was wrong to try to make you into something you're not. I guess I was just carried away by a lot of silly fantasies."

Joe didn't say anything, but his expression encouraged her to go on.

"If you did what I wanted you to do, you wouldn't be you. And it's you that I care about. Just the way you are."

Was she making any sense? The slow smile that grew across his face told her he understood.

"That's all I want," he said. "Carrie, I—I've missed you." He paused as if he wasn't sure what to say next. Then he seemed to make a decision. "Carrie, I love you."

And Carrie had no problem at all responding. "I love you, Joe."

Joe took Carrie's hand. "May I have this dance?"

Carrie smiled. She felt as if she were flying above the crowd. "Why, I'd be delighted."

And as they moved back onto the set, Carrie knew, with complete certainty, that Joe was a thriller, too, in his own special way.

We hope you enjoyed reading this book. All the titles currently available in the Sweet Dreams series are listed on the next two pages. They are all available at your local bookshop or newsagent, though should you find any difficulty in obtaining the books you would like, you can order direct from the publisher, at the address below. Also, if you would like to know more about the series, or would simply like to tell us what you think of the series, write to:

Kim Prior,
Sweet Dreams,
Transworld Publishers Limited,
Century House,
61–63 Uxbridge Road,
London W5 5SA.

To order books, please list the title(s) you would like, and send together with your name and address, and a cheque or postal order made payable to TRANSWORLD PUBLISHERS LIMITED. Please allow cost of book(s) plus 20p for the first book and 10p for each additional book for postage and packing.

SWEET DREAMS NON-FICTION